LISA RYAN CAMPBELL

Ex Appeal

THE *ex* FILES

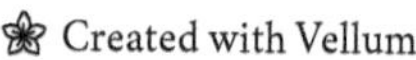 Created with Vellum

PROLOGUE

*F*ive years ago…

Ava pulled her deputy vehicle to a stop in front of the Hideaway River cabins. The moment she switched off the ignition, the pelting rain against her windshield rose to an almost roar. Why did murder fit so well with a cold and rainy night?

She raised the hood of her jacket and got out of the car. Stuart, a fellow deputy of Gypsy Bay met her at the entrance of cabin number five that now had yellow crime scene tape covering its door.

"Two bodies," Stuart began as Ava stepped up to him. "Male and female. The male has three GSW's to the chest, the female has two."

Ava looked around the empty lot as raindrops poured over her hood. "Were they the only residents?"

"There are a few other guests according to the manager. He said he was surprised they checked in on a night like this and figured they were tourists who got off the beaten path."

"Did he hear or see anything?"

Stuart shook his head. "I grilled him pretty good, but he stood firm. I'm guessing the murderer used a silencer."

"If so, then this couldn't be random." She stayed quiet for a moment, dreading her next question. But it was why she was there in the first place.

"Is it her?"

Stuart hesitated, then nodded somberly. "Her wallet in her purse verifies her ID, but I recognized her as soon as I saw her."

Ava gave a brusque nod and indicated she was ready to go inside. Stuart ducked under the yellow tape and lifted it up for her to follow in after him. The smell of death assaulted her as soon as she stepped over the threshold and into the cabin. She covered her mouth and turned to Stuart who read the silent question in her eyes.

"The coroner will have to do a full autopsy, but from the looks of them, I'd say they've been here for as long as she's been missing," he said.

Three days. Her husband had waited the full twenty-four hours before reporting her missing, so she could have possibly been dead for four days.

Ava stepped past the open living room and into the bedroom. She moved in closer to the bed, risking her senses and slid on latex gloves. The two bodies were sprawled across the bed with their clothes removed. Michelle Meyer was down to a green lace bra and matching panties, the bra now stained with dark red blood from the fatal wound to her chest. Her companion was in his boxers, his eyes opened and fixed on nothing.

"Who's the guy?"

Stuart pulled out his small notebook. "He had a wallet, too. Christopher Foster of 3317 Chastain Lane. Again, we'll have to get next of kin to verify."

He lived here in Gypsy Bay, too. Ava could only imagine

the rumors that were sure to fly. Her coastal hometown wasn't so small that everyone knew each other's name, but it was not so large that a random scandal could just fall through the cracks. And what they had here was definitely a scandal.

* * *

Ava and Stuart pulled up to the single-family ranch home on the quiet street. She looked at the clock on the dash then up at the house. A few lights were on inside.

"It's after two in the morning," Stuart said, frowning. "What's he still doing up?"

Ava shrugged and once again raised the hood of her jacket to protect against the rain that had yet to let up.

"Michelle's been missing for four days," she said. "He's probably worried sick."

"From what I've been hearing about their marriage, I doubt that."

Ava gave him a look before leaving the car. "Forget town gossip."

The two made their way up the porch steps. Ava put her finger to the doorbell, hesitated for only a moment, and then pressed it. This was the shittiest part of her job, and it only made the circumstances worse that she knew the next of kin —intimately.

Several seconds passed before they heard footsteps from inside. Finally, the door opened, and Gabriel Meyer stood there fully dressed in casual attire, pinning her with his dark green gaze.

"Mr. Meyer, I'm sorry to disturb you so late—"

"Is this about Michelle?"

Ava was taken aback by his sharp tone and then quickly recovered. "Yes. May we come in?"

"Just say what you need to say."

She hesitated, but the look in his eyes told her to get on with it. "We found her inside a cabin off the US-17 bend. She's dead."

"Was she with someone?"

"Mr. Meyer—"

"Dammit, Ava, don't spare my feelings! Was she with another man?"

"Yes."

He nodded once and then slowly closed the door in her face.

CHAPTER ONE

*P*resent day

She wasn't alone out here.

For the last two weeks, Ava had been saying that to herself. With the weather getting slightly warmer, at least as warm as it could get for northern California and visitors making their way to Gypsy Bay, her morning jogs through Strawberry Woods were no longer her own. More often, she was giving the obscure head nod as a greeting to fellow joggers she passed and a 'hello' or 'good morning' to others. Some were even bold enough to halt her in her run to ask about the best places to eat in town or where to find the most spectacular view of the Pacific Ocean. Of course, she would indulge them. Every happy tourist was a boon to Gypsy Bay's economy, and happy tourists meant less calls to which her and her fellow deputies responded. However, the advice she gave tourists was always attached with the disclaimer that she had been away for five years and that she was getting reacquainted with the town herself.

But this intrusion in her morning run was different. She

could always sense when she was about to pass someone or even if someone was behind her. If the latter was the case, she'd simply stop, step to the side of the path and kneel down to feign tying her shoelace. Ava didn't like the feeling of being chased. However, she couldn't decipher whether the person on this trail with her was either behind her or coming at her—but someone else was definitely out here.

She continued her run, deciding whoever it was would show themselves eventually. This trail, although hidden in the denser area of the woods, was clearly defined. City officials had put mile markers along the way, not only for those wanting to track their progress, but to also give a sense of security, assuring a hiker or jogger that they hadn't wandered off the trail and were lost.

She felt herself travelling uphill now. Soon, she'd be rounding the curve that would take her past the overlook of the river. On instinct, she began to speed up, just as she had been doing every morning for a week since she'd returned to Gypsy Bay. She didn't want the memory of what she saw here to assault her and figured just running past it as fast as she could would keep it at bay.

As she came near the familiar pass, she quickened her pace until she was moving at a dead run. She rounded the bend, and just like every time, she kept her head forward, ignoring the flowing river down below and the trees surrounding the grassy area. The bend was a quarter mile long, and everyone loved to stop there on their hike or run through the woods. Ava used to love it too, and it was one of the things she missed most when she lived in Los Angeles. But now, she kept pushing, running from unwanted memories.

A scream went up in the air, shattering the silence and Ava turned in alarm, still running as fast as she could. With that momentary lapse in focus, she didn't see the man who was standing just a few feet in front of her. She plowed into his hard body and together they fell to the ground.

"Shit," the man ground out from beneath Ava's weight. He'd broken most of her fall, but she still felt dazed.

"I'm so sorry," she said, over and over as she gingerly lifted herself off of him and rose to her feet.

Reaching down to give him a hand, she got her first full look at his face and froze. So did he.

"Gabriel."

He looked into her eyes and then ignoring her outstretched hand, rose to his feet and full height. He took a second to dust himself off and then looked at her for a long time. Ava took him all in.

Even after five years spent apart, she still wasn't prepared to see him. What she couldn't deny was that the sight of him still made her heart flutter. He had changed over the years, growing into a strikingly handsome man. He had cut his dark hair, the low cut prevented her from recognizing him at first, and she also noted his close-shaven jaw line that gave her a view of his full lips. But his signature feature were the intense sea-green eyes that always had a powerful effect on her. With him, being so close to her, they were even more hypnotizing that she practically fell into a trance and nearly stumbled again. But he quickly reached out and grabbed for her elbow to steady her.

"Thank you," she said, breathing hard from her now racing heart.

"You were going pretty fast. Didn't you see me?"

No, she didn't, but she sure as hell felt the impact. He was older, but he'd grown stronger and fully muscled.

"I heard a scream. I thought..." She trailed off, looking down toward the clearing and searching for what had distracted her.

She began to breathe easier when she saw it was just a

group of teenagers playing around. She watched as the tall blond boy lifted the screaming and now laughing girl in the air, feigning to throw her in the river, while their friends stood by laughing at the scene.

"I see tourist season is still a big hit around here," she said.

"They're probably local kids. We were the same way growing up. Remember?"

She turned to him, but didn't answer. Back then, she didn't run in his same crowd. She was a trouble maker, a fast girl, the kind nice boys like him didn't associate with. But somehow, that didn't stop them from finding their way to each other.

"What are you doing here, Ava?"

The question threw her off guard and she stared at him, stupefied. "You know I like morning jogs."

"I mean, what are you doing back here in Gypsy Bay?"

She looked up at him, refusing to be intimidated. "I'm sure with town gossip being what it used to be, you may know I'm working for the sheriff's office."

"And reopening Michelle's murder investigation."

She wasn't going to get into this with him out here. The moment she crossed the city line into Gypsy Bay, she promised herself all encounters with Gabriel Meyer would remain professional.

"If you want to talk to me about it, come by the station." She put her earbuds in. "I have to go."

"Going is what you do best," he called after her, and she pretended to not hear the parting shot.

When she felt sure she was far enough away from him and the clearing, she moved in front of a large tree and sank to its trunk. She pulled her knees up to her chest and dropped her head to rest against them, trying to get her breathing under control. She wasn't easily rattled, but seeing

Gabriel for the first time in five years and in those woods disturbed her peace of mind. Now, the memories she warded off were hitting her with full force, and as painful as they were, she was going to have to face each and every one of them.

CHAPTER TWO

Gabriel pulled into the parking lot of the sheriff's station, turned off the ignition and leaned his head back against the headrest. He tightened his hands around the steering wheel and breathed in and out several times. He hadn't expected this reaction after seeing her, but he only had himself to blame. He'd heard she'd moved back to Gypsy Bay a week ago. Gabriel didn't know if over the five years her interests and hobbies had changed, but took a chance that running was still one of them and that sooner or later, she'd return to what had once been her favorite trail in Strawberry Woods.

It took him a few mornings, but finally, this morning, he'd timed her run correctly. He trailed behind her about a half a mile, noting how slender but still very curvy her body shape was. Her narrow waist curved into full hips and a round, firm ass that had his dick jumping at the thought of the things they used to do together. He couldn't see her front, but imagined her breasts were still full and luscious just the way he loved. But fantasizing about his ex-girlfriend's body was not why he'd gone out there, and it pissed him off to know she still had an effect on him. He'd come out to the woods to corner her for answers. Namely, why after all these years, did she suddenly make an appearance?

He was familiar with the trail she was taking and knew that eventually, she'd come to the hillside by the clearing where a beautiful view of the river could be seen. Gabriel took a shortcut, rounded the path and got to the clearing before she did. He took a minute to admire the view, but underestimated just how fast she would be going. As it happened, he found himself on the ground beneath her, and yes, even in a sports bra, he could see and feel that her breasts looked just as delectable as he'd remembered. Even more erotic, they'd both been sweaty from running, and her body had felt hot and sticky beneath his hands.

Damn! She was still beautiful. Still the same attractive Ava Beckett he had fallen in love with years ago. The Ava Beckett he thought would become his forever. However, she had other plans, which turned out to be walking out of his life without a heads up. After she left Gypsy Bay, he wallowed in misery for a while, but at the urging of his father, he focused on his studies, his career and in finding someone that would aid in his rise in politics. That had been Michelle Kingston and the Kingston family name. With his marriage to her, he thought he was finally moving onward, only Ava had returned, finished her schooling and became a deputy with the sheriff's office, and Gabriel realized he was never truly over her.

Then Michelle was killed, and with God's sense of humor, Ava had been in charge of the investigation. He remembered how he had to endure countless questions from her and the other deputies and spent many nights wondering if the woman he secretly loved would also be the one who arrested him for murder.

They called it a crime of passion, and after months of

searching for the killer, the investigation had been relegated to the cold case files, and Gabriel felt both pain and relief. Relief, that for now the whispers and rumors had ceased, and pain, because Ava chose that moment to leave Gypsy Bay for good.

Now, five years later, she had once again returned, the investigation was being reopened, and she was at the center of it all. It was like letting out the rotten smell from an extracted coffin, awakening memories that he had tried hard to subdue.

Seeing her again this morning brought back memories of when they were still lovers—the way she would smile at him, her curly hair that felt soft to his touch, her gorgeous brown eyes that burned with sheer curiosity, and the taste of her lips that when he kissed her, told him that she was all he needed. Looking back now, he realized how pathetically in love he'd been with a woman who turned out to be a money-hungry opportunist.

With his desire for her temporarily squelched, he climbed out of the car and strode to the entrance of the building. He nodded to many of the deputies he knew and recognized, not just from his work at City Hall, but because he'd gotten to know many of them well, following the days after his wife's body was found in a lakeside cabin along with her lover.

Once inside the sheriff's office, he approached the front desk and greeted Sheriff Spencer's assistant, Jennifer.

"Good morning, Mr. Meyer," she said, smiling.

He returned the greeting with a smile of his own. "Is the Sheriff in?"

Before she could reply, Gray Spencer, a tall, well-built and imposing man filled the doorway of his office. He and Gabriel were about the same height, only Gabriel was more lean than muscular.

"Come on in, Gabe," Gray said, flashing that easygoing

smile that Gabriel was convinced had been part of the reason he would have no trouble getting re-elected. The other reason had been his now very pregnant wife, Shannon who spent long days, weeks and months campaigning for her husband's re-election. Coupled with his reputation of being a fair and honest man, it had all worked because the people of Gypsy Bay loved Gray and his and his wife's love story.

Gabriel admired and respected the man as well. Gray Spencer had come from old money, but he never let that privilege interfere with his duties and work ethic. He had heard through town gossip that after Gray and Shannon remarried, he sold the mansion that once belonged to his parents, and the two of them moved into a smaller, yet spacious lake house they refabricated.

Gabriel envied the family and home they made together, and decided it was time he made plans to move out of the home he and Michelle shared. The memories were a mix of good, bad and mostly indifferent. The sad truth was there hadn't been any love in their home—only an arrangement.

"Have a seat," Gray said, indicating one of the visitor's chairs. "I assume you're here about Michelle's case."

Gabriel nodded. "I saw Ava this morning. I know you reopened the investigation."

Gray neither acknowledged nor denied the statement. He simply braced his elbows on his desk, resting his chin in his clasped hands, staring at Gabriel with a knowing look.

"I want to know if there's anything I can do."

"You've done everything asked of you. Your wife's death and the investigation happened while I was still a deputy, but since I got this job, I've been going through the cold case files and I wanted to see if maybe there was a chance that we could close some of these cases out. I saw you made a list of any friends, associates and enemies. You answered all questions and were very forthright. Since I'm reopening the case, you'll be notified if there's anything else we need from you."

"Any suspects yet?"

"No. I assigned the case to Deputy Beckett, because she was the lead investigator on it before. She's committed to it. If you have any questions, I can give you her card." He paused. "She made quite a reputation for herself in Los Angeles after catching the Rivergate killer. Plus, she's a local. She knows the town and the people. Trust me, she's a competent deputy, and I have a lot of faith in her."

"You don't have to defend her to me. I didn't say anything."

The knowing look returned as Gray sat back and rested his hands on the arms of his chair. "I'm not one for listening to town gossip. I've had my share of it when my brother died and Shannon…well, you know the story. But I know you and Ava have a history. Is this going to be a problem?"

"No."

Gray studied him for a moment longer, his eyes hard and unmoving as if he could see right through the lie. Gray Spencer might have grown up as Gypsy Bay's rich kid, but all that money had nothing to do with the man he had become. He was a cop through and through with a cop's instincts.

"Okay, so maybe there will be some conflict of interest."

"How?"

Gabriel splayed his hands. "We used to date."

"That was years ago."

"I know how long ago it was."

"You think your previous relationship will cause her to act unprofessionally?"

"That's not what I'm saying."

"Look Gabe, before the investigation went to the cold case files, I remembered how hard she worked on it. She reviewed the evidence, she issued the search warrants, she did everything to the best of her ability," Gray said. "Now that she's back, I want her on the case again to see if anything new can be found."

Gabriel wondered how he could make the Sheriff understand that he didn't want his ex-girlfriend heading the investigation into his wife's murder. He felt like he was losing his mind, and not from grief, but from the woman who was back in his life. He had gone from pretending she didn't exist to having her presence thrown in his face at every available opportunity. What angered him most of all, was that each time he set eyes on her, he didn't think about Michelle. He thought that if Ava hadn't left him in the first place, he wouldn't be a murder suspect.

Gray must have sensed his frustration, because he leaned forward and spoke with genuine concern.

"Gabe, do you want to find your wife's killer, or not?"

CHAPTER THREE

After her run, Ava drove around the downtown area, and could see that over the years, many businesses had ventured into the sleepy coastal town. It still had the sense of a quaint small town, but Gypsy Bay was definitely gaining popularity with those who were ready to escape the bustling life of San Francisco and other larger cities.

She noticed too, that along the corners of the streets were posters sporting smiling faces of men and women running for local office. With her move, new job and everything else going on in her life, it had slipped her mind that this was an election year. She drove by the City Hall building and saw a crowd gathering on the steps. Atop the steps was a podium and behind it, Ava recognized the handsome face of Jake Lacey who stood proud and orating to his crowd of constituents. She slowed down and saw his wife, Samantha Lacey smiling and clapping at the appropriate times in his speech. Ava remembered he had been elected County Commissioner just before she left Gypsy Bay. Now, it appeared he was campaigning for his second term.

She continued past the crowd toward the sheriff's office,

but slowed to a stop at the light. She looked around once more at the busy streets of patrons and those on their way to work. Her gaze swept over more campaign posters and then halted when she came to another, much more familiar face. He was wearing that same self-assured, dashing smile for the camera. His dark brown hair was cut short, and his hard jaw and cheekbones accentuated his handsome face. The camera didn't do his eyes justice, though. The green tinge was slightly there, but standing directly in front of him, they were simply mesmerizing.

A horn honked impatiently behind her, and she realized she was holding up traffic now that the light had turned green. As she sped away, she recalled the line on the campaign poster just below his smiling photo.

Elect Gabriel Meyer for County Commissioner.

* * *

Ava couldn't help but feel a sense of comfort as she walked up the porch steps of Tess's home. They were the quintessential BFF's, and Tess always had a way of making Ava feel calm and centered whenever she was near. She hoped she did the same for her.

They met at a math camp while in middle school, and immediately became the best of friends. Tess was the numbers genius, and Ava was the curious girl who simply liked solving puzzles. They thought they were incompatible until one afternoon at camp during a hike, Ava rescued Tess from falling into a ditch, and it cemented their friendship. And as was custom with best friends, the two women entrusted each other with their deepest secrets. As it stood, Tess was the only one who knew why Ava had left Gypsy Bay and walked out of Gabriel's life.

"Coming," Tess's deep voice sounded from inside the house.

Ava chuckled to herself. In school, Tess used to hate the tone of her voice, because being an alto meant she was singing with mainly boys in the school choir, whereas Ava and the majority of the girls sang soprano. Now, as a grown woman, Ava noticed how men seemed to fall into a trance at the sound of Tess's sultry melodic voice, although Tess pretended not to notice. When the woman opened the door, she grinned at the sight of Ava at her doorstep.

"I know you just came from exercising, but I made cookies."

Ava groaned and stepped inside the large five-bedroom, four-bathroom Victorian home that served as both a bed and breakfast and Tess's home.

"Only one," Ava said, eyeing her. "And I mean it."

"Coffee?" Tess offered.

"Thank you." Ava took a seat in the large sitting room.

In moments, Tess returned from the kitchen holding a tray with a plate of chocolate chip cookies and two mugs of steaming coffee.

"I know I've said this before, but I'm so glad you're back," Tess said, handing her a mug of coffee. "I never thought I'd see you in Gypsy Bay again."

"Why?" Ava asked, gingerly sipping from her mug.

Tess sat down on the sofa across from her and cocked her head to one side. "Are you serious? You haven't been here for five years, and whenever you had a vacation and wanted to see me, I came to L.A."

"There's more for us to do in L.A.," Ava protested.

"Oh yeah? Well, there's more to do in L.A. than Phoenix, but you didn't have a problem visiting your parents."

"They're my parents," she countered, laughing. "They don't get around as easily as they used to do."

"Admit it, Ava. You were purposely avoiding this place."

Ava took another sip and shrugged her shoulders. "Maybe a little. So, what of it?"

"So, it begs the question: Why did you move back?"

Ava sighed loudly. "Okay, L.A. was becoming a bit too much for me. That big city—all that murder—I just couldn't do it anymore. I missed this place, and I missed you."

Tess made the shape of a heart with her hands against her chest.

"Well, I see you made a name for yourself out there," she said, grabbing a Los Angeles Times newspaper from behind her. On the front page was a picture of Ava speaking at a press conference with the headline that read:

LAPD Detective Catches Rivergate Killer.

Ava groaned. "Where did you get that?"

"Where do you think? From your mom. I think she ordered every edition they had and sent them to everyone," Tess smiled. "I'm proud of you."

"Thanks, but that's one of the main reasons I left. Working that case nearly killed me with all the man hours my team and I put in. So, when I saw my little hometown was looking for a new deputy, I applied." Ava narrowed her eyes at Tess. "Do I have you to thank for getting me the job?"

"Trust me, the second you told me you were applying, I marched right down to Sheriff Spencer's office and demanded he throw away all other applications and just hire you. But it turns out, I wasted my time. He already made up his mind to give you the job. Your reputation precedes you."

Ava shook her head, smiling, and the two of them lapsed into a momentary silence until Tess finally cleared her throat.

"I know you want to ask me, but you won't, so I'm just going to tell you. He's doing well. He's running for office this year, he's healthy and currently not seeing anyone."

Ava rolled her eyes. "Thanks, but I was downtown this morning and saw he was running for office, I definitely don't need to know about his relationship status, and for your information, we already ran into each other—literally."

Tess raised one eyebrow in anticipation of a good story. "So, you two finally saw each other. How did that go?"

"Great, considering that he looked like he wanted to plunge a knife into my chest."

Tess tucked a strand of hair behind her ear. "Well, that's a little dramatic."

Ava shrugged. "I don't know how else to describe it. The man hates me."

"I don't think so."

"He doesn't know why I left, and I hurt him. I really did."

They fell into another silence and Ava stared into nothing. As far as she could see, she'd returned to the town she left long ago to pursue an investigation that involved a man she used to love. What had she been thinking in even applying for the deputy position? She'd been thinking she missed her home, Tess—and although she'll never admit it aloud—Gabriel. There was no way Gabriel wouldn't hate her. Hell, she hated herself for what she did.

"Are you going to tell him?" Tess asked, breaking the silence.

"What would be the point?" Ava asked.

"It may help him understand why you left."

"I left because I was paid off. End of story."

Tess didn't push further, sensing Ava didn't want to continue the topic and smartly changed the subject.

"So, the Sheriff put you back on your old case, and you're here to find out who killed our town's beauty queen and her boyfriend."

Ava groaned. "If I'd known why I was hired in the first place, I may have just stayed in L.A."

Of all cold cases to put her on, Sheriff Spencer had put her on the case of Michelle Meyer, Gabriel's wife. Five years ago, she had been found shot to death in the Hideaway River cabins along with Chris Foster; a man with whom it had been rumored she was having an affair. Ava remembered conducting a thorough investigation, considering the status of both Gabriel and Michelle's families. They'd both come from the small elite group of Gypsy Bay's wealthy community. However, even with the political pressure put on the department, a suspect was never apprehended.

Tess smiled sympathetically. "You made a name for yourself up there, and we're all lucky to have you back."

"I'm not sure others will share your sentiment once this case gets underway."

Ava reached into her bag and pulled out a file. Tess watched her as she did so, stretching her hand to take a picture Ava handed to her.

"She was a beautiful woman," Tess remarked, studying the photograph of a smiling Michelle Meyer, "and it's about time the truth comes out."

"That means I'll have to tell what I saw."

"You mean the two of them arguing and then making out by the river?"

"She was dead a week later, Tess. Maybe if I had come forward when I saw that—"

"It was a private moment between a husband and wife. You couldn't have known what was going to happen to her, and please, stop blaming yourself for what happened between you and Gabriel."

"I ran away from this place and from him like a coward."

Tess leaned forward and spoke with finality. "You were scared. You didn't think you had any other choice, and it's not like Gabriel…"

She paused and Ava frowned. "It's not like Gabriel…what?"

Tess sighed. "It's not like Gabriel was waiting around for you to come back. You were only gone for eight months, and he'd already moved on with Michelle."

"Yeah, I know," Ava said, taking the picture back from Tess and staring at it. Michelle Meyer had been beautiful, a model with the eyes of an angel. In the picture, her sleek black hair fell over her shoulders, complementing her smile.

"She was perfect for him."

CHAPTER FOUR

The next morning, Gabriel walked past his assistant, Diana and into his office, closing the door behind him. He didn't make it a habit to keep his door closed, but this morning, he woke up frustrated and didn't want to risk taking his dark mood out on his staff.

He sat down at his desk, leaned back in the chair and stared up at the ceiling. It was starting again. Word had spread like a brushfire that the murder investigations were being reopened and Gabriel was getting the same looks, the same whisperings and the same flawed notion that he could be responsible for Michelle's and Chris's deaths.

He remembered the rainy night when Ava and another deputy came to his home to inform him of his wife's death. He even remembered feeling nothing, even as he dragged himself to the morgue to identify her body and the numbness as he stared down at her eyes, that were still open in fear.

It was a sight Gabriel would never forget, and he'd spent many nights to follow drinking heavily to make himself return to that numbness in order to escape the pain, because despite the reasons they married, she was still his wife, and she was an intelligent and beautiful woman who didn't deserve what happened to her. Then, there was also the guilt that plagued him whenever he thought about his decision to divorce her that night he followed her. That was also the same night she was killed.

He recalled evenings she would come home, smelling faintly of a man's cologne. Michelle didn't love him, and they seemed to understand that the marriage was one of opportunity and a way to satisfy their families. However, to the public, they were in love and the perfect, blissfully happy couple.

But once news of Michelle's death had circled, along with the fact that she was found naked in bed with Chris Foster, the people of Gypsy Bay saw him as a jealous husband who viciously murdered his wife and her lover.

The sheriff's department had been very careful not to come right out and say that he was a suspect, but he knew how these things worked. Michelle was rich, beautiful and apparently having an affair. His motive had been practically gift-wrapped for the deputies, and the only reason he hadn't been arrested all those years ago, was because there was no evidence directly linking him to the murders.

He thought for a moment and plotted his next steps. He didn't want to sit back and wait for the sheriff's office to come to him with new developments. If he was going to finally put all of this to rest and move on with his life, he needed to take charge. He was going to look for his own answers into Michelle's death, and even if he couldn't find the murderer, he could at least find evidence that it wasn't him.

Gabriel rose to his feet with a plan in mind and at the same time, someone knocked on his door.

"Who's there?" He called impatiently.

"Diana."

"Come in."

She swung the door open, smiling warmly as she held a tablet to her chest. Diana was a lively lady, one of the few people he liked working with, but today, he wasn't in the mood for her jokes or a rundown of his morning agenda.

"Good morning, Mr. Meyer. You have a meeting with Jake Lacey's campaign manager in thirty minutes."

Gabriel stalked to the coat hanger and shrugged on his jacket. "He wants to offer me an executive staff position in hopes of me dropping my bid for election. Save him the time and trouble and tell him forget it."

"Okay," she said, suddenly flustered and looking down at the tablet. "I'll go ahead and cancel the meeting. You also have—"

"Cancel everything else for this morning and reschedule with my apologies. I need to run an errand and probably won't be back until after lunch."

Without another word, he walked past her out of the office, ignoring the curious looks of his staff.

CHAPTER FIVE

Carmen Foster, the widow of Chris Foster, lived in an upscale neighborhood in Gypsy Bay, not far from Gray Spencer's family mansion. As Gabriel walked into her expansive home, he wondered why Chris had chosen to risk all of this and sleep with his wife. Everyone in Gypsy Bay had talked about Chris and Carmen's grand wedding. It was a memorable event, held in one of the largest and oldest chapels of the community.

By all appearances, Chris and Carmen had been in love. So, when the news of his death and alleged adultery came out, it had tainted the couple's loving image. Gabriel knew what that felt like. Familial and societal expectations ran rampant in his family, too. He and Carmen shared the bond of having to hold their head up in a town that believed they were nothing less than perfect.

"I was wondering when you'd finally come here," Carmen said, as she led him into an open sunlit sitting area of her home.

She looked gorgeous, dressed in a peach-colored cocktail dress that revealed her feminine curves. Her makeup was light, perfect enough to not shield her natural beauty, and she wore her hair down, its blonde tresses nearly reaching her waist.

"Going somewhere?" He asked.

"Yes, a friend's birthday party in the city," she said, gesturing for him to take a seat.

He nodded, unbuttoning his suit blazer and taking a seat in an armchair. "I won't be long. So, you were expecting me?"

"As soon as I heard the rumors that Ava Beckett had returned to Gypsy Bay, bringing her stellar reputation as a Detective with her, something told me Sheriff Spencer would assign her to the town's most famous cold case. It was after all, her case."

She paused and sent him a secretive smile. "Didn't the two of you used to be serious?"

The question brought him out of his thoughts like a lightning strike, and suddenly he was remembering a past before Michelle. And just like always, those memories turned into carnal images he had no business remembering. Ava, naked and laughing beneath him and then the laughs turning to moans and pleas as he bent over her and gently took one of her breasts into his mouth.

"A long time ago," he said, quickly and forcefully slamming the door shut to any more recollections of her.

Carmen must have sensed he didn't want to expand on the subject and politely steered the conversation back to the matter at hand. Still, he could read the question in her eyes: *Why did she leave you?* It was the same question everyone wanted to ask, and he couldn't blame them, because it was what he asked himself over and over again for five years. But the only one who knew the answer was Ava.

"Has she come to question you, yet?" she asked.

"I've been avoiding her," he admitted.

Except on mornings when she jogged through the woods, and I hoped to catch a glimpse of her.

Carmen sighed. "I know you came here for answers, Gabriel, but I can't think of anything more to tell you that I haven't told the sheriff's office. Chris left that night after dinner, telling me he had an appointment to show a house to a client. That wasn't unusual. Chris worked around his clients' schedules all the time, day and night."

"Did you notice anything strange when he returned?"

"He walked through that door as drunk as a skunk, which wasn't like him at all. I tried to get him to talk to me about what was bothering him, but he only lashed at me and told me to mind my own business. So, I had Gina help me put him to bed. When I woke up the next morning, he was still snoring away, so I ran errands. When I came back that afternoon, Gina told me he left and didn't say where he was going or when he'd be back."

Gabriel remembered reading in the police report a witness statement from a bartender confirming that Chris had indeed been drunk. The bartender cut him off and sent him home.

"You never suspected—"

"No," she cut in. "He was too stressed about money to have an affair. Chris's mother was in a rehab facility for her back, and her insurance was only covering part of it. Frankly, I was glad to hear he was still getting business, because we were up to our necks in medical bills and other debts." She paused to look around the opulent room and its decor. "We weren't the best money managers. Gina quit six months ago, because I couldn't afford to pay her anymore, and I'll probably need to sell this place to keep myself afloat."

Gabriel nodded, feeling sympathy for her. The fantasy she'd built for herself was crumbling to the ground.

"Is there anything else you can think of, and please try to

think hard, Carmen. This second time may be our only chance of catching whoever did this."

She shook her head, sadly. "I've told you all I know. It was only after his death when I found out about his relationship with your…with Michelle. She was rich and beautiful. Maybe he thought leaving me to be with her would ease his mind financially and give him a comfortable life."

Carmen leaned back in her chair, intertwining her fingers and stared at Gabriel with curiosity.

"Why don't you leave this for Ava to handle? Don't you trust her to do her job?"

"I want to find out who did this."

"Or, you're more interested in clearing your name."

Gabriel gave her a look, but Carmen dismissed it by laughing.

"Don't worry, I've had my share of the accusations," she said and began to mimic the rumors circulating about her. "'She's rich, so she could have hired someone to kill them. She found out about their affair and killed them both in a jealous rage.'"

"I really am sorry about this," Gabriel began. "I know you'd rather forget and just get on with your life."

She nodded. "I thought I was finally getting that chance. Then when I heard the case was being reopened, I knew it was going to start all over again. I'll admit I called the Sheriff and gave him an earful, but then I immediately felt bad about it." She paused to chuckle sardonically. "Ava is only doing her job, and…"

She trailed off and Gabriel knew what she wanted to say. Chris had been found dead, in bed naked with Michelle, and it was difficult for her to drum up sympathy for her murdered and cheating husband. It was the same conflicting feelings he had for Michelle. She had chosen to be disloyal to him in life, so was it so wrong for him to feel the same way towards her in death? The answer to that was yes, if it made him look guilty of murder.

Carmen quieted and looked away to a far spot across the room. "Still, I never suspected for a minute he was cheating on me. I mean, Christ, in a town like this, you hear rumors, you know who's doing what and with whom."

She stopped abruptly, looked at him and then glanced away quickly as a horrified look came over her face.

"I need to get back to the office," he said, also standing and saving her from her embarrassment. "I appreciate you talking to me."

He turned to leave the room and headed towards the foyer, hearing her heels against the tile floor as she trailed behind him.

"Gabriel?"

He stopped at the front door and looked back at her, his hand resting on the door handle.

"You should know Ava was here yesterday, asking a ton of questions."

He nodded. "That doesn't surprise me. She'll probably want to speak to everyone again who was involved in the case."

"Well, I expected her to ask me the same questions you had—about Chris and the last time I saw him alive. But she didn't."

He removed his hand from the doorknob and turned around fully to face her, feeling that fight or flight sensation rise within him. "What did she ask?"

"She asked me questions about you, like had you ever threatened Chris in any way, had I ever seen you threaten Michelle, and if I'd seen you around town the day of the murders." She paused. "I don't want to alarm you, but I get the feeling she may be eyeing you as a suspect."

* * *

His anger was already simmering by the time he returned to his office, but seeing Ava and a few of her deputies only made his mood darken. By the time he came upon her standing at the receptionist's desk, he was baring his teeth.

"What the hell is going on?"

Ava remained calm, cool and as steadfast as ever despite the storm he was bringing to her, and it made him want to throw something. She'd always been able to do that and rarely allowed him to see any kind of emotion play across her features. It made him feel unsure around her. What was she thinking? What was she feeling?

"I need to speak with your staff, one by one. They will be simple, routine questions," she said, her demeanor still composed. "We don't plan to take up any more of your time than necessary."

Gabriel glared at her for a moment longer, and without another word, he stalked past her and into his office, slamming the door behind him. He would allow Diana to deal with Ava and the other deputies, while he got on with his work.

But when two hours had passed, and he hadn't made a single phone call or returned one email, he came to the conclusion he wasn't going to be able to concentrate—not with her only several feet away.

CHAPTER SIX

By late afternoon, the staff interviews were complete. The office began to close up, and all of the men and women had gone home, including Gabriel's assistant, who checked in on him before leaving. The two deputies who'd accompanied Ava had returned to the station, and now, it was just her and Gabriel in the office, separated by a closed door.

She stood at the door, breathed in and out several times and braced herself for what waited for her on the other side. She needed to get this interview over with, but she also didn't want to deal with his temper. He likely believed she was looking at him as a suspect, but that wasn't the truth at all. It was important to her to eliminate him as quickly as possible and continue on with her investigation.

She raised a closed fist and knocked on his office door. When she didn't receive an answer, she slowly turned the handle, opened the door and stuck her head inside.

"Mr. Meyer?"

He was sitting at his desk, staring into his laptop screen.

When he heard her voice, his eyes slowly slid over to her, and then back to the screen without a word.

"We've finished interviewing your staff, and it looks like everyone has left for the day. I wanted to thank you for your cooperation."

He nodded. "Just close the door on your way out."

Ava breathed in and out slowly and stepped fully into the room, ignoring the irritated look in his eyes when he saw she didn't leave.

"Actually, Mr. Meyer, I have one more interview to do, and that's with you."

"We've already gone through this before. Five years ago. Why don't you go through those files and review my statement? I can assure you nothing has changed."

"A lot can change in five years," she replied. "You may know and recall more than you think."

Gabriel switched off the computer and stood. He then went to the corner of the office where a coat rack stood and snatched his coat from it.

"Whatever you say, but let's make it fast. I have somewhere to be in fifteen minutes."

Ava chewed the inside of her jaw. He was really testing her patience, but it was what they did to each other. He got angry, she stayed calm, and he pushed her buttons just to see if he could bring her to his level. However, she was determined not to give him what he wanted.

She turned and took a seat on the sofa in the corner of his office, pulled out her notepad and pen and rested them on her lap. She then fixed her eyes on him firmly, indicating that this interview would last as long as it needed to.

Gabriel appraised her like a formidable enemy on the battlefield. He then slipped on his coat and then leaned against the edge of his desk and motioned for her to begin.

"First, I'd like you to tell me everything you remember

about the day of Michelle's death. I know it was five years ago, but do your best."

"The only time I saw her was during breakfast. We said a few words to each other, she kissed me goodbye and said she had appointments and errands. We sometimes met for lunch, but on that day, she said she wouldn't be able to meet. That was fine with me, because I had a full day of meetings scheduled here at City Hall."

"Did you two call or text one another throughout the day?" Ava asked. "Maybe a 'hello', 'how's your day going', or 'I love you' kind of thing?"

She kept her head lowered to her notepad when she asked the question. Truthfully, she didn't want to hear about their day to day lives, but it was all essential to track her whereabouts that day. When he didn't respond for a while, she dared herself to look up and found him watching her, strangely.

"We didn't have that kind of marriage."

He continued to stare at her, and she wondered if he was thinking the same thing as her. Periodic text messages and phone calls throughout the day were something the two of them used to do when they dated.

Ava cleared her throat. "So, you didn't see her at all that day. What about the evening? Were you concerned when she didn't show up for dinner?"

"As I said in my first statement, I was working late that night, too. Again, Michelle and I hardly checked in with one another. It wasn't until I got home a little after eight and saw that she wasn't there that I got concerned. That's when I texted her. I called her a few times, but by eleven that night, I started to grow worried. She'd never stay out that late."

"You called the sheriff's office," Ava assumed.

"Yeah. They told me to give it until morning, since she was an adult, and I did. I didn't sleep that night and by morning, when she hadn't yet come home, I called back and declared her missing. That's when I heard that Carmen Foster also made a call that her husband hadn't come home that night, either."

"After coming home from work, did you happen to leave the house at all the rest of the night, for any reason?"

"No."

She was absolutely certain he was lying. But why?

He grabbed his keys off the desk and jangled them in his hands. "Anyway, you know the rest. Chris and Michelle were found in a lakeside cabin, naked in bed, both shot to death. The rumors started spreading that they were having an affair, someone found out and killed them both. Of course, only Carmen and I would have motive to kill them for that, but no evidence against either of us was found."

He paused and narrowed his eyes at her. "Do you think I killed her?"

"No."

He threw up his arms with impatience and anger. "Then why are you questioning Carmen about me? Why are you interviewing my staff? Are you going to search my house again, too?"

"I'm conducting an investigation."

"And it sounds like the focus of your investigation is on me."

"You were the closest one to her. I just need to find something to clue me into what she was thinking and what she was doing the day she was killed."

"Find anything?"

"Just one," she sighed. "There's evidence your wife was planning to leave you."

Gabriel stilled. "What do you mean she was planning to leave me? What evidence?"

Ava pulled out her cell phone and checked the clock

display. "Maybe we should continue this tomorrow. Didn't you say you had somewhere to be?"

"It can wait. I want to know what you found out."

"It was just a hunch," she began. "But something didn't feel right to me about her movements the day she was killed. You said she had errands and appointments to keep, but why is it that no one remembers seeing her around town that day?"

"Maybe she went out of town. Maybe she went all the way to San Francisco."

"I guessed that and checked the toll booth records. Michelle's car was never recorded going into the city. I checked other traffic cams in the surrounding areas of Gypsy Bay, and she wasn't seen anywhere—except one place."

"Where?"

"A lawyer's office."

"A divorce lawyer?"

"No. An estate lawyer." She flipped through her notepad until she came to a page of scribbled notes. "Miguel Sanchez. He was in charge of managing and distributing her trust fund left to her by her parents."

"I paid a visit to him, and he told me Michelle came to him, begging him to release $75,000 on advance to her. He reminded her of the restrictions of the trust, and that she couldn't receive any of it until her thirty-fifth birthday."

"What did she want it for?"

"Mr. Sanchez said she wouldn't tell him, but she appeared distressed. She became visibly upset when he wouldn't release the funds and threatened to sue him before leaving his office."

"And you think she wanted this money to leave me and take Chris to start a new life somewhere?"

"So far, it's the only explanation that makes sense." She

paused. "Sanchez tells me you received the balance of the trust after her death."

He groaned. "Yeah, as if I needed more of a motive to kill her."

She let that hang in the air for a moment and then spoke softly.

"Did you ever suspect Michelle was having an affair?"

He shrugged. "I guessed something was going on from her behavior."

"Did you ever confront her about it?"

"To be honest, Ava, I didn't care."

She narrowed her eyes. He looked like he cared a lot from what she saw in the woods that day.

"How could you not care? She was your wife."

"Maybe in name only."

She closed her notepad with a snap, tucked it away and stood. "Thank you for your time, Mr. Meyer, and I guess that's what happens when you marry a woman after only eight months."

She regretted the words as soon as she said them. She regretted them even more when she got to his office door, opened it, and he was there slamming it shut again and looking at her with triumph and anger in his eyes that came dangerously close to exploding.

"There it is," he said, invading her space. "That's what I've been waiting for. You may be fine with walking around like there's nothing between us, but I'm not. Yeah, I married her after eight months. So what? Where were you?" He paused and then snapped his fingers in her face as if just remembering. "Oh, that's right. You were too busy cashing that $250,000 check my dad gave you!"

Ava tried to shove him out of the way in a desperate attempt to escape, but she only managed to pry the door open an inch, before Gabriel slammed it shut again. She tried once more to push him out of the way, but he must have been waiting for her to make that move. As she barreled into him, he encircled his arms around her waist, trapping her within his strong embrace.

"Gabriel—"

He overpowered her and silenced any further protests by leaning down and covering her lips with his own, delving his tongue inside her mouth. It was a shock to her system to have his lips on hers after so many years, but it was feeling so much like homecoming. She pressed her closed fists against his chests, silently begging for him to stop before the sensations took hold and her body betrayed her. But she was well past that, and her struggles against him gradually ceased.

Gabriel let go of her arms, and immediately, Ava put her hands to his shoulders and slipped his coat off and encircled his neck with her arms. He shrugged his coat off the rest of the way, let it fall to the floor and once again brought his arms around her waist to bring her closer to him. They moved with each other, moaned with each other, tasted each other and explored each other. She reacquainted herself with the delicious feel of his lips and the hard, rigid frame of his upper body, and she wanted so much more.

"Oh, God. Gabriel," she said, breaking the kiss to catch her breath.

He put his hands to the sides of her face and kissed her a few more times before staring into her eyes.

"Was taking that money worth it?" he asked. "Was it worth throwing away what we had?"

And just like that, her fantasy came crashing down. She pulled herself free of his grasp and pushed him away from the door. This time he didn't resist but backed away and allowed her to leave.

CHAPTER SEVEN

Five years ago…

On this crisp, early February morning, Ava expected to pretty much be alone in the woods. But someone else was out here. The thought kept invading her mind as she ate up the miles in her run through the trail. The sound of dry, dead leaves being crushed under her sneakers were muffled by the earbuds she wore, but she distinctly heard a man shouting.

Ava slowed to a stop and removed the earbuds. It was definitely a man's shout, followed by a woman's angry reply. So, there were two people out here sharing her solitude, and from the sound of things, she was about to intrude on an argument. She knew this trail like the back of her hand and realized once she rounded the curve, she would come to a clearing where the river ran. If one didn't watch their step, one could trip down the steep hill and fall into the water below. Ava was coming to the clearing now, and the voices were escalating.

She saw the two of them and immediately ducked back into the trees. They were directly across from her, just on the other side of the river. Ava was on a hillside above them, but the woman was facing the wooded hillside, and if she happened to look up, she'd see Ava. But Ava could definitely see her and recognized her on the spot.

It was Michelle Meyer—a very enraged Michelle Meyer, staring up at her husband, Gabriel with murderous eyes.

"You really think you're going to leave me and run off to be with him?" Gabriel asked, and looked to be barely containing his fury.

"I told you I'm not in love with him," she said. "It was a mistake to get involved with him."

"You know if this gossip got around, my career would be over. Did you even think about that?"

"I said I'm sorry! I didn't mean for it to go this far."

"If I get backlash from this, it's over between us."

His reply was muffled, but there was bite to it. Ava risked a peek from behind the trees and tried to study him. From behind, she recognized his height and build, and although he wore a black baseball cap which shrouded his eyes, it looked a lot like Gabriel.

"I hate you!" Michelle spat. "You would love for me to be humiliated, wouldn't you? Well, guess what, honey? If they talk about me, they'll surely talk about you."

He said something to that, and it earned him a slap that made Ava wince. She started to turn away, uncomfortable with the violence and the fact that she was witness to such a private moment but stopped just as he started to turn away. Something inside her wanted to confirm it was Gabriel. However, Michelle tugged him by the forearm, turned him back around and clasped his face between her hands. She said something, but her soft words were disguised by the sound of the flowing river and then she kissed him fully on the lips. He seemed to go rigid at first contact, and then a few seconds later, he wrapped his arms around her waist and drew her in to deepening the kiss.

This time, Ava did turn away. Gabriel and Michelle's marital concerns were none of her business, and the last thing she wanted to do was watch her ex-boyfriend passionately kissing his wife. She retraced her steps back through the woods, deciding her morning run was over. But, as she neared the end of the trail where her car was parked, she heard a scream.

Her head whipped around back to the entrance of the dense woods. Without another thought, she ran full speed back into the woods and returned to the clearing. Her heart was racing, afraid of what she might see. But, when she got back to the clearing and focused her eyes where Gabriel and Michelle, there was no one there. Just the flowing river and an empty patch of grass where the couple had been standing.

* * *

Ava put the glass of wine down and leaned forward on her couch to rest her head in her hands. It wasn't the first time the memory of seeing Gabriel and Michelle by the river replayed in her mind. She should have detailed the incident in her report years ago when she was first assigned the case, but the argument and that scream…it all made him look guilty.

Then her thoughts drifted to this afternoon. Why the hell did she let him antagonize her like that? It was his oldest trick, and she fell for it! He wanted to see her come apart and that's exactly what she did. And then he had the nerve to kiss her. She picked up her wine glass again and swallowed the rest of its contents in one gulp. She couldn't do this.

She set the glass down and for about the fifth time, she picked up her cell phone to call Sheriff Spencer and ask to be removed from the case, but just like the previous times, pride stopped her—pride, determination and a commitment to see this through. Her reputation in Los Angeles is what got her on this cold case, and there was nothing about her that was a quitter. She'd just have to find a way to endure Gabriel and the memories he conjured.

She gazed over at the 8x10 photograph of Michelle Meyer lying on her coffee table. Picking it up, she sat back against the sofa and studied the image of the beautiful brunette with hazel eyes that Gabriel chose to be his wife, eight months after Ava walked away from him. She tried her best to focus on what was important by asking herself who would want her dead and why. But she kept staring at the photo, remembering Michelle as the straight A, college-bound and outgoing teenager, whereas Ava herself, had been the elusive, bad girl who always seemed to stay in trouble. She now recognized her teenage antics as that of a girl desperate to be seen and heard. But underneath that prickly exterior, she was just a regular adolescent girl vulnerable to the smile of one of the school's adolescent guys.

While they were in high school, he constantly asked her to go to the movies with him, to a concert with him, and God forbid, even to the prom with him. She ran with a tough, rebel crowd back then, to her parents' dismay and always carried around a chip on her shoulder for no reason. It scared most people away, namely the good girls and guys, which was her goal. But to Gabriel, it seemed as if her "bad girl" image made him more determined to make her his. Despite her small attraction to him, Ava continued to rebuff him and tried to get him to understand that they were out of each other's league. After they graduated, she found her own identity, lost track of the rebel crowd. She saw Gabriel around town a few times, but she was too focused on completing her criminal justice degree, and he seemed to have found an interest in politics. In any event, she figured he'd gotten the hint and moved on.

Then on a chilly Christmas Eve, years after they graduated high school, Gabriel strode into a seedy bar where she worked. She and the other patrons took one look at him and his friends and figured they were just out slumming. A bunch of rich, white guys home for the holidays and looking to get into something. But when he walked into the bar and saw her making and serving drinks, Ava both mentally rolled her eyes and swooned, because he was staring at her as if no time had passed between them and they were still in high school where he was completely smitten.

"You're on the wrong side of town," she said, handing him the beer he ordered. "You'd better get back home before it gets dark."

He smiled, took a swig of his beer and watched her over the rim with those sea green eyes she had to admit she loved and missed.

He put the glass down. "I'm right where I need to be."

It had gone on like that for most of the night. The subtle back and forth like chess, each with their own different endgame. But, by the time she closed up the bar, Gabriel's friends had deserted him, the regular patrons had gone home, and he was walking her to her car with her number stored in his cell phone.

"I'm no good for you, Gabriel."

"Why don't you let me be the judge of that," he said, and punctuated that with a kiss.

When their lips parted, they stared at each other, both obviously wanting to take whatever this was between them further.

"I know what I want, Ava. And it's you."

He'd worn her down, and he kept wearing her down as the months went on in their courtship, and for nearly two years, they lived in a fog of bliss.

Then Paul Meyer paid her a visit.

CHAPTER EIGHT

"You're quiet this evening," Paul said, reaching for his glass of wine. "Anything on your mind?"

Gabriel looked up from the steak and carrots on his plate. Not for the first time, he wondered why they continued to have these dinners together. They never talked about anything except their respective careers, and once that topic was exhausted, they fell into an awkward silence and eventually ended the evening with a polite goodbye.

But his father continued to request he join him for their weekly reservation at an upscale restaurant on the outskirts of the city where they held the same private table in the corner. Gabriel agreed solely out of respect for his father, but his heart was never in it.

"I'm sure you've heard they're reopening Michelle's case," Gabriel said, taking his cloth napkin and tossing it onto his plate. "I just figured that was all behind me."

"There's more bothering you than that," Paul said, narrowing his eyes. "You can handle town gossip, but this is an election year, and of course, your ex-girlfriend decided to move back to town."

"She's got nothing to do with my mood."

"Doesn't she?" Paul said and added under his breath, "I wonder how much she'll take this time to leave town."

Gabriel saw red, but instead of disrespecting his father and telling him how he really felt, he rose, grabbed his coat from behind his chair and put it on.

Paul sighed and grabbed for his hand. "I'm sorry, that was out of line. Please, Gabriel, sit back down."

He looked around the restaurant, eyed the exit and then looked to his father. Finally, he sat down, but kept his coat on.

"I didn't realize you still had a soft spot for her," Paul said. "Again, I'm sorry. I just wish this wasn't happening for you at this crucial time. Like you said, it was all behind you—the scandal Michelle caused this family, it was dead and buried along with her. Now, that Beckett woman is back to bring it all up, while your head should be focused on winning the County Commissioner seat."

Gabriel began to smile with derision.

"What is it?" Paul asked.

"Doesn't it strike you as funny that the woman you wanted me to marry was the one who caused the greatest problems to my career and this family?"

"So, she fooled me. It wouldn't be the first time I was wrong about a woman." Paul chuckled. "What? You think Ava would've been a better choice in a wife for you? Come on, Gabriel, the two of you were so young and immature. She tended bar, and you were barely getting into politics. She was a distraction."

Gabriel shrugged. "Maybe we were young, but we're not young anymore and we're both pretty successful in our careers."

"Yes, I heard she was a big shot detective in L.A. and caught that serial killer that even the FBI couldn't catch,"

Paul admitted, and to Gabriel's ears it sounded begrudgingly. "It doesn't mean she was right for you."

"I guess we'll never know, will we?"

"Listen, you know the lawyer's number. Give him a call if it starts to seem like she's focusing her investigation on you."

Gabriel waved a hand away. "I'll be all right, Dad."

He wanted to say he could handle Ava, but that was years ago, when she didn't mind letting her guard down around him. Too much time had passed to the point where she now seemed to be a stranger, and he wasn't sure where he stood with her anymore. That afternoon, however, had been the first time he saw a chink in her armor. Damn, her lips tasted good. It was as if the anger he'd been harboring towards her instantly vanished the moment she was in his arms. The way she molded against him, the way she moved with him, God, it all felt so fucking right, and it had taken every ounce of strength for him to let her just walk out of his office. Now, not only did her face and smile occupy his mind, but her body as well, and that could only mean trouble for him.

CHAPTER NINE

va hoped to God Gabriel had taken his jog earlier this morning, but to be safe, she'd put off her own run until late afternoon. The last thing she wanted after that searing kiss and those angry words yesterday was to have another encounter with him here in the woods.

She raced through the trail, challenging herself to beat her record, but in reality, she was running away from that kiss, the things he said, and the memories it brought up.

Was it worth throwing away what we had?

As much as those words pissed her off, a voice whispered somewhere deep inside that throwing away their relationship was exactly what she'd done.

* * *

Gabriel resembled Paul Meyer very much, except in height. His father was an inch or two shorter, but they had the same dark hair and same shade of eye color that seemed to peer into her soul.

"Can I get you anything?" Ava asked as he pulled up a barstool and looking very out of place in the establishment.

"Water will be fine," Paul said.

Ava nodded, turned to pour him a glass of ice water from a pitcher and sat it in front of him.

"Thank you," he said, taking a sip and looking around the place.

"So, what can I do for you, Mr. Meyer? I just spoke with Gabriel before I started my shift, but he's okay, isn't he?"

"Oh, yes, he's fine. But this isn't really about Gabriel. Well, in a matter of speaking, it is, but I came here to talk about you." He paused. "I had a routine doctor visit today and I saw you in the same medical complex. Dr. Perry, right? He was my wife's OB for many years before she died."

Her heart began to slowly pick up speed. "That's right."

"I guess I don't have to tell you that I have ways of finding out information, and what I found out was both surprising to me and alarming."

"I don't understand."

"My son is very fond of you, and I can see why," Paul said, his eyes trailing her with what appeared to be reluctant respect. "You have a mysteriousness about you that is very desirable."

She didn't say anything, wondering where he was going with this.

"The other side of the coin is I believe you're very fond of him, too. Only, you have a secret you've been keeping from him."

"I don't know what you're talking about."

"I'm sure you know exactly what I'm talking about," he countered, his eyes going directly to her abdomen.

Ava began to tremble with anger at the man's audacity to use his wealth to get information about her. "Did you tell him?"

"No."

"Then, I'd appreciate it if you let me tell him. With all due respect, this is between Gabriel and me."

Paul pulled an envelope from inside his jacket and placed it on *the bar counter. "What would you say if I wanted to keep it between you and me?"*

"What's that?" she asked.

"Enough to give you a new life. I tried talking to Gabriel, but for whatever reason, he refuses to see things my way. But something tells me you're a smart woman and not so easily taken in by matters of the heart."

"Even if this is love between you two, you can't possibly think it will last. When it doesn't, what will you have left? Nothing. Face it, my dear, this is just a false life you've been living. Take the money and give yourself a better life. Do you think Gabriel is going to halt his dreams to be with you?"

* * *

She should've thrown that money back in his face, told him to get lost and then called Gabriel and let him tell her to her face whether he wanted her or not.

Her favorite spot in the trail opened up before her, and unlike usual, where she'd run past the clearing, this time she stopped to take in the view and revel in the peace it gave her. Maybe Tess was right. She should tell Gabriel the truth, even if she blamed herself for what happened between them. She at least owed him an explanation.

The faint sound of crunching dead leaves underneath a sneakered foot jolted her out of her thoughts, but before she could turn around, she felt strong hands push her from behind, sending her at full speed down the hill. Her scream became inaudible to her ears as she tumbled over and over down the hard earth. But in her moment of terror, she managed to catch sight of a shadowed figure standing at the hilltop, watching her plummet to the ground.

CHAPTER TEN

$\mathcal{A}$va's eyes flew open to a white-washed ceiling and fluorescent lighting. Unsure of where she was, she tried to sit up and almost immediately, pain like no other shot through her body and she groaned aloud.

"Easy there. Easy."

She had closed her eyes to the pain ricocheting through her, but then jolted them open at the familiar voice that she used to find so much comfort in hearing. When she pried opened her lids and stared into the same eyes and face she used to love, she wasn't sure anymore if she was now staring at an enemy.

She allowed him to ease her back down to the pillow, because for the moment, laying down was the only position that felt good to her aching joints. But once she was situated, she moved away from his touch and looked up at him with a narrowed gaze.

"What are you doing here, Gabriel?" she asked, her voice sounding raspy to herself.

He frowned, obviously sensing her change in mood. "I heard about your accident. The Sheriff is on his way. A hiker heard you scream and found you at the bottom of a steep hill. What the hell happened? You could've been killed."

She tried to think back, but could only recall a shadowed figure standing at the top of the hill watching her. The height, build and stature told her it was a man, but he was wearing dark clothes and a baseball cap low that shielded his face. She would never be able to positively identify him.

"I—I don't know," she said. "I was thinking about..." She paused and looked up at him.

"You were thinking about what?"

You, me and that stupid deal I made with your father.

"Just a bunch of things, and all of a sudden, someone just pushed me."

"Did you see who it was?" Gabriel asked.

"No, but..." Her words got lodged in her throat as she took in his stance, his physique and the dark sweats he was wearing. The only thing missing was a black baseball cap.

A throat cleared, and the two of them looked to Gray Spencer, standing in the doorway of her hospital room.

"May I come in?"

"Of course," Ava said. "Thank you for coming, Sheriff."

"I'd rather not be visiting one of my deputies in the hospital," he said, coming forward to place a hand on hers. "How are you feeling? We heard you had quite a fall."

She tried to sit up again, and this time was aided by both men until her back was propped against a pillow. "I was doing my daily run through Strawberry Woods and someone pushed me down a hill."

Gray's brows rose in alarm. "You're certain they pushed you? They didn't just accidentally run into you?"

She shook her head. "I was lost in my thoughts while I was running. Sometimes, my music helps me do that. I stopped for a moment, zoned out for a while, and all of a sudden, I felt someone's hands against my back and a hard shove that sent me over the hill."

"Jesus," Gray muttered.

"Someone followed her out there," Gabriel spoke up. "It's Chris and Michelle's murderer."

Gray turned his gaze to him, and Ava looked at him with irritation.

"We don't know that," she rushed to say.

"Yes, we do," Gabriel said, ignoring her glare. "You usually run in the morning, but this time you ran in the afternoon, and someone just happened to be there at the same time. They were following you." He turned to Gray. "It's this investigation. She's obviously getting close to the truth, and the murderer is trying to stop her."

"You don't know that," Ava said. "Still watching a lot of crime tv?"

"Is this true?" Gray asked. "Do you normally jog in the mornings?"

"Yes," she said.

"Everyone in this town knows you jog that trail in the mornings," Gabriel insisted. "Everyone knows your routine."

"Including you," she said.

"What's that supposed to mean?" he asked.

Gray sliced a hand through the air and turned to Ava. "Why did you switch your routine?"

Ava looked past the Sheriff to Gabriel who looked to also be waiting for her answer. "I...got bogged down in the case files this morning, and just couldn't find the free time until late afternoon."

Gabriel wasn't giving up. He tried once again to appeal to Gray. "Sheriff, take her off this case. She's in danger."

"From who?" Gray asked, slowly.

"If I knew who, I wouldn't be standing here," he said. "I'd be at the son of a bitch's house and handling this myself."

"Gabriel, stop!" Ava exclaimed.

"All right, take it easy, both of you," Gray said, calming the tension in the room. He divided a look between the both of them, and then settled his attention on Ava.

"Look, I'm not one to panic easily, but Gabe may have a point. You're running a cold case investigation in which a murderer was never found, which means he or she is still out there. This morning, you were pushed down a steep hill by someone you claim stood there watching you. That doesn't sound like just some random attack."

"As long as she continues this investigation, she's not safe," Gabriel gritted.

"Sheriff, you put me on this, because I was the lead investigator before, and because you have confidence in my ability," Ava said. "I'm making headway, and I'm not about to be scared off by some coward who's afraid I might be getting close to the truth."

She swung her eyes over to Gabriel who was all but seething. "I'm not dropping the investigation."

Gray sighed but regarded her with subtle admiration. "That's good enough for me. Take a few days off to recover, though, and let me know when you're ready to get back to it."

She nodded with a smile. "Thank you, Sheriff. I'll have a full statement for you by the morning."

Gray looked down at his watch. "I need to get home. I don't like leaving Shannon alone for too long this late in her pregnancy." He then took another look between them. "Goodnight, both of you."

"Goodnight," Ava said.

"Sheriff," Gabriel said and nodded to him as his imposing presence left the room.

When they were alone, Ava nervously brought her hand to her neck and realized her necklace was missing. She had a habit of fiddling with it while thinking, but it was now gone.

"What's wrong?" Gabriel asked.

"Nothing. Will you hand me my clothes from the chair over there?"

"You're leaving?"

"Yes, it doesn't feel like I broke anything. I want to go home, take a nice long bath and sleep in my own bed."

He nodded and handed her clothes to her. "I'll go ask for your discharge papers and send in a nurse to help you get dressed."

She looked up at him, hesitant to feel any sense of gratitude toward him, especially after what transpired between them only a day ago. But she never could resist his kindness, even when she didn't feel she deserved it.

"Thank you."

He nodded awkwardly and left the room. Apparently, neither of them was used to this sudden warmth between them. In a few minutes, a nurse with a pleasant smile on her face came into the room.

"I hear you're ready to get out of here," she said, unfolding Ava's clothes and laying them across the bed.

"Yes."

"Well, you're very lucky. We ran several tests and didn't find any broken bones or fractures. You just need to give your body a few days' rest."

She helped Ava move her legs to the side of the bed and step into her jogging pants. Next, came her sports bra and finally her shirt. By the time, they were finished, Ava was breathing heavily from exertion.

The nurse handed her the fanny pack she carried while running, and she immediately began to dig through it, searching for her lost necklace, but came up empty-handed.

"Lose something?" The nurse asked.

"I was wearing a necklace when I was running, but I guess it must've fallen off when I fell down the hill."

She looked up from her fanny pack. "You didn't happen to see it with my things, did you? It's a thin, white gold chain with a single lapis lazuli gem."

The nurse shook her head, tossing wisps of her hair in different directions. "No, nothing like that. The hiker who found you, brought you in here with only your clothes and pack."

"Okay. Thank you for your help."

She smiled. "No problem. Someone should be right in with your discharge paperwork."

Ten more minutes passed before she signed her paperwork and was ready to leave, and she was not surprised when Gabriel insisted on taking her home. However, she was much too tired and sore to argue with him, so she rode in the passenger seat of his car in silence until they arrived at her two-bedroom cottage on Cherry Street. He helped her out of the car, and she tried not to react to the feel of his hands at the small of her back as he guided her to the porch and finally to the front door. She gave him her keys, and he unlocked the door and gestured with one hand for her to proceed him inside. She stepped inside her home and suddenly the living area felt very small with his presence.

She instantly turned to face him. "Thank you for getting me home, but I'll take it from here."

"I'm checking the house and the surroundings to make sure everything is secure. Whoever that asshole was could've followed you home."

"I can do that."

"Not in your condition. Go upstairs, run your bath, and I'll make you something to eat before I leave."

"Gabriel, please!"

"What?" He exploded. "What is it?"

"I need you to go home. You being here could compromise my investigation."

"Why? Because I'm a suspect?"

"Yes!"

He stilled and the two of them shared a look, mirroring surprise at her outburst.

"No," she amended. "I mean—I don't know. I just can't have you here."

He looked around as if he wanted to pick something up and throw it. "I can't believe I have to say this to you, but I didn't kill Michelle or Chris."

"Then let me do my job and prove it. That means not interfering with my case or trying to get the Sheriff to reassign me."

"I won't apologize for caring about you."

"But this is my job."

"I don't give a shit about that job. I just want to talk to you."

"About what?"

"What do you think? About us!"

"Christ, Gabriel, there is no us, because that's all over."

"It's over because you fucking ended it!" His voice rose to a shout. "Five years ago, you ended it, and I didn't get a say. You just took the money and ran."

"And you moved on."

"You call this moving on? Me, trying to catch a glimpse of you doing your morning jogs and remembering how we'd jog that trail together? Me, dropping everything as soon as I heard you were hurt? Or me, these past five years wondering how insane it would be for me to book a flight to L.A. and come find you?"

He came toward her in a flash. She started to back away, but he grabbed her hand and slapped it against his chest. "You feel that? I haven't moved on at all. You're still here in me."

She could feel his heart racing, and wanted to tear her

hands away, but he kept them there and tears came to her eyes at the thought of the all the pain and wasted years.

"I'm sorry. I wish I could make you understand."

He kept one hand clutched over hers and used his other hand to brush away one lone tear that managed to fall. Ava closed her eyes at the feeling of his touch and felt Gabriel lean his forehead against hers.

"I missed you," he whispered. "I fucking missed you so much."

She felt his hand move to her waist and bring her closer to him. His touch was like fire, and as much as she wanted and needed for it to continue, she had to remember her promise to herself and not cross that line with him.

"Gabriel," she said, taking a step back.

"I know," he said, releasing her. "I'm sorry."

They shared a look of regret and longing before she turned away and slowly began to make her way up the stairs.

"You can lock the door on your way out."

He nodded. Good night."

Ava had only made it up a few steps before she turned back around. "Gabriel?"

After that confession, Ava thought it was only fair to confess something of her own. She didn't want another day to go by without him knowing how she felt. He was already at the door but stopped and turned. His green eyes pierced her, as if trying to guess what she wanted to say.

"I never wanted to leave you."

Without waiting for his response, she turned and continued up the stairs to her bedroom.

CHAPTER ELEVEN

*H*e should leave. He really should turn around, walk through that front door and lock it behind him without looking back. His mind kept insisting that's what he do, but his feet and his heart didn't agree.

He didn't want to leave her. After five years of her being gone, she was once again in his sight, back in his life, when for a while he accepted he'd never see her again. He even began to move on with his life, entertaining subtle and even overt flirtations from other single women in Gypsy Bay, concentrating on his career and making goals for himself to rise in public office. He was even making plans of starting a foundation with the money from Michelle's inheritance for missing children. He was moving on. He was, and now she was here again, bringing in the past with her like a tsunami.

I didn't want to leave you.

After all these years passed, she wanted to tell him that? She could've said that in an email or better yet, she could've told his father to go fuck himself and to keep his fucking money. Why had it been so hard for her to fight for them when it hadn't been hard for him? He remembered a conversation he'd had with his dad about her.

"You could do better than her, son," Paul said.

"No, I really can't. She's the best for me," Gabriel said.

That had shut the entire conversation down. Maybe it was then his dad had sensed he couldn't wrangle his son to do what he wanted, so he went looking for easier prey. But never in his wildest dreams did Gabriel ever think that Ava would succumb.

I didn't want to leave you.

He headed towards the rear of the small house. He didn't care how much she insisted he leave, he was going to do a check around her home before leaving, starting with the back patio and making his way to the front. But as he passed the spare bedroom, he realized she must have turned it into her home office. The door was open, and what he saw inside brought him to a full stop.

Tacked to the wall opposite her desk was a large poster board that was basically a visual representation of his wife's murder investigation. Stapled to the center of the board were two 8x10 photographs—one of Michelle and one of Chris. From the pictures, she drew red marker lines to more photos of their closest relations, friends and places they were last seen. Then, she listed suspects, and there was only one photograph circled multiple times in red marker.

He closed the office door and did a check around the inside and outside of her house. When he assured himself she was safe, he programmed the automatic lock on the door to secure it behind him, got in his car and drove home.

I didn't want to leave you.

Did she still have feelings for him? He couldn't be sure, but God knew he still had feelings for her, which was laughable considering it had been his photograph circled in red.

He was still in love with a woman who suspected him of murder.

CHAPTER TWELVE

*S*unlight streamed through the curtains of Ava's bedroom window, and the moment she turned over, her aching muscles screamed in protest. She cried out, instantly regretting not taking that hot bath last night.

"Good morning," a voice rang out.

She rose her head slightly and saw Tess striding into her room with a glass of orange juice.

"Hey there, friend," Ava said with a smile and a groggy voice.

She remembered giving Tess a spare key when she first rented the home, but as she sat up in bed and looked around the loft, something else plagued her.

"He's not here," Tess said, guessing at the question in her mind.

She handed her the glass of juice and sat on the side of the bed. "He left some time last night, but called me and told me what happened. I promised I'd come by to check on you."

Ava nodded, taking a sip of the juice. She groaned in pleasure the moment its chilled liquid touched her sore throat.

"I can't believe someone just pushed you like that. You

could've been seriously hurt. Hell, with those steep hills in those woods, you could've broken your neck!"

Ava patted the air between them before Tess really got upset.

"It's okay. I promise I'm fine." When she tried to adjust her sitting position, her muscles screamed again, and she let out an involuntary cry of pain.

"Oh, yeah," Tess said, rolling her eyes and taking the glass from Ava. "You're in great shape. Come on."

"Where are we going?"

"I'm helping you get out of bed and into the hot bath I've got waiting on you. Then I'll make you some breakfast."

The thought of steaming water, scented bath salts and bubbles followed by Tess's fluffy and cheesy eggs brought tears of relief to Ava's eyes. She looked up at her friend with open gratitude.

"God, I love you."

Tess laughed.

* * *

After a long, hot bath and breakfast, Ava and Tess chatted while doing some stretching exercises together. Finally, Tess had errands to run and although Ava was grateful for her friend, she was relieved at her departure, because she had her own stuff to do. Namely, track down a murderer who had just made their first mistake by coming after her.

The drive to Strawberry Woods didn't take long, but the hike to where she'd been pushed did. She had to move slowly and cautiously, without overdoing it and giving her body a chance to heal. By the time she got to the spot where she was pushed, she was winded and perspiring. She knelt down at the peak of the hilltop and looked over to where she'd fallen. It was a steep hill, and if her assailant had used a bit more strength, she could've broken something. Were they trying to kill her or just scare her?

An undetectable noise and the feeling that someone was behind her alerted her, and after what happened yesterday afternoon, she was on full attack mode. She instantly stood from her kneeled position and whirled around with her gun already drawn.

"Whoa! Whoa!" Jake Lacey halted and raised his hands in alarm. "I'm sorry, Deputy. I didn't mean to scare you. It's Ava, right?"

"Commissioner Lacey," she breathed and sighed, tucking her gun into the back waistband of her jeans. "Yes, my name's Ava. What are you doing out here?"

He slowly lowered his hands. "I sometimes come here to get away from all the day to day. It's peaceful. Just the wind, the trees and the river."

She nodded, still studying the man. She never got to know him or his wife, Samantha, personally. She'd only seen him around town or in paid advertisements for his run for County Commissioner. It was odd seeing him in the flesh now, when for so long she'd only seen his picture on billboards.

"By the way, I found this and wanted to return it to you."

Jake dug into the front pocket of his jeans and removed what looked like a small, white gold necklace. She stepped closer and held out her hand, instantly recognizing the tiny blue gem that was now cracked but still winking up at her from the sunlight.

"Where did you get it?"

He slowly dropped it in the palm of her hand. "I found it earlier when I began my walk along the trail." He hesitated. "I heard about your accident."

She frowned and he shrugged. "You know how this town is."

"Yeah, I know how it is," she said, tucking the necklace into her pocket. "But it wasn't an accident. Someone pushed me."

Shock blanketed his face. "You're serious?"

"Yes." She started to look around the trail and then down at the river.

He must be really getting desperate."

Ava turned back to him with another frown. "What are you talking about? Who's desperate?"

"Gabriel Meyer, of course. Ever since that murder investigation was reopened, people around here are saying he's been acting strangely and not like himself at all."

She nodded. "Well, it's understandable. Michelle was his wife. It can't be easy for him or Carmen Foster."

"Sure, but from what I can tell, he hasn't once mourned her passing. He buried her and seemed to dust his hands free of her. This is horrible to say, but it seems to me he was relieved when she died."

She didn't know what to say to that, but could recall the night she and Deputy Randall visited Gabriel and broke the news of Michelle's death. No, he didn't look distraught, but she attributed that to shock. As the weeks and months passed, she'd been too focused on the investigation and keeping it out of the cold case files to observe Gabriel's grief process.

"I'm actually glad I ran into you," Jake said, bringing her attention back to him. "I know you're heading the investigation again, and I was going to call you or come by the station. I met a man at one of my rallies, and he told me something interesting about the night Michelle and Chris died."

"What did he say?" she asked.

He spoke with hesitancy. "If it's all right, I gave him the number to the sheriff's office and your name. What he has to say…you're going to want to hear for yourself."

CHAPTER THIRTEEN

Five years ago…

"You keep looking at your phone," Paul said, stabbing his fork into mashed potatoes.

Gabriel put his phone face down on the table. "Ava left for Phoenix over a week ago, and she hasn't called or texted me yet."

"I'm sure she's fine." Paul put his fork down and reached for his glass of wine.

"Even if she is, it's not like her to not call." He shoved the food around on his plate. "I think I'll call her parents just to make sure—"

"Gabriel, I said she's fine!"

He frowned at his father's sharp tone. "How would you know?"

"Because she has $250,000 in her pocket."

"What are you talking about?"

Paul leaned back in his chair with exasperation. "I warned you about her, didn't I? I told you that you could do better than her, and I was right. Your girlfriend took the money, ran and she's not coming back."

"You're lying," Gabriel said. "Ava wouldn't take your money. Why would she?"

Paul shrugged. "Who knows what her reasons are."

"I don't believe you."

His heart told him she wouldn't do that, but he kept thinking about the day, one week ago, when he dropped her off at the airport. The way she looked at him so strangely. The goodbye. It felt final. Now, every call and text to her was going unanswered. What was he supposed to think? What the hell was going on?

* * *

Gabriel was reviewing the minutes from the last city hall meeting when his doorbell rang. He left his home office and made his way to the front door. He swung it open, and at the sight of her, all of his thoughts ceased. He started from the top, noticing how unlike the times she wore her hair in a bun at the nape of her neck while on the job, it was now down her back and framing her face with its soft waves. Gone was the deputy uniform to be replaced by a waist-length jacket and a gray, snug-fitting tank that clung to her breasts and gave him a view of her cleavage and creamy brown skin. The jeans she wore weren't tight, but molded to her body and showed off her thighs and—if she turned around—her full, plump ass. She was dressed casually, and he assumed she didn't come over here to tempt him, but the sight of her was driving him crazy.

"Hi," she said. "I went by your office, and your assistant told me you were working from home today."

He nodded, not trusting himself to speak just yet.

"I wanted to thank you for your help last night in making sure I got home okay. And, thanks for calling Tess."

When he only nodded again in acknowledgment, she

took a tentative step closer to him, which in his mind, was very dangerous. She was investigating him for the murder of his wife. If he just kept telling himself that, maybe the urge to snatch her by the waist, pull her into the house and fuck her on his couch would eventually pass.

"But I think it's best if we continue to keep things professional between us."

Gabriel saw red. "Is that really why you showed up at my door? To tell me we're keeping this professional?" he asked, staring at her with eyes that bore his growing rage. "Sure, let's keep it professional while you're busy stacking the deck against me."

"What?"

"I saw your murder board yesterday in your office. I'm your number one suspect."

She closed her eyes, and he knew she was trying to cling to her patience. "It's not what you think."

"Then what do I think? What is the truth?"

"You have the biggest motive, yes, but I'm trying to prove you didn't do it! I figured I owed you that much," Ava blurted, and he was almost certain she hadn't meant for that last sentence to slip.

A sarcastic laugh burst from him. "Why? Because you're feeling guilty for leaving?"

"My reasons don't matter. The point is that I can't eliminate you as a suspect if you don't start talking to me."

"What do you want to know?"

"How did you feel when you found out Michelle was having an affair?"

Irritation flooded through him. "We've been through this already. I told you I didn't care if she was or wasn't having an affair. We didn't love each other like…"

Like you and I loved each other.

Ava stared, and he got the distinct feeling she could read his thoughts.

"What about your career? Surely, an unfaithful wife wouldn't bode well for a man with political aspirations."

He shrugged with indifference. "I'm sure it wouldn't."

She huffed out an exasperated breath, threw up her hands and turned to walk back to her car. Her patience was completely gone, and that's the way he wanted her, because in that state, she stopped pretending and spoke from her heart.

Gabriel reacted instantly. He came away from the doorway and stalked out onto the porch. She didn't make it but a few feet before he stepped in front of her, blocked her escape and towered over her.

"What's your problem?" he hissed.

"My problem is you and that you won't stop lying to me!"

"I'm not lying. I really didn't care that she was having an affair. I would've been relieved if she had been, because it meant our fake marriage was over."

She glared at him with fire in her eyes.

"What is it?"

"I saw you, Gabriel. I saw the two of you in the woods a week before she was killed, and you were confronting her about her lover, so yes, you very much did care!"

He reeled back as though she had slapped him, and the look he gave her was nothing short of confusion.

"What are you talking about?"

"I was doing my morning run through Strawberry Woods. I stopped at that clearing on the trail that overlooked the river. The two of you were there, arguing."

He was still confused, and the look on his face must have been more than she could take.

"Really? She shouted. "You're really going to stand there, looking at me as if I'm speaking a foreign language?"

He took hold of her arm and brought her close to his face. They were surely giving his neighbors a show, but he didn't give a shit.

"Listen to me! I don't know what you're talking about. I never argued with Michelle in the woods at any time before she died. You're mistaken."

"I'm not mistaken," she gritted. "I know what I saw."

"Then whoever you saw, it wasn't me."

A tense beat passed, and he didn't like the trace of suspicion still in her eyes.

"Ava," he reiterated. "It wasn't me."

She held his gaze for just a moment longer and then wrenched her arm free of his grasp. "Okay."

He looked up at the sky and noticed clouds forming, but they could just make it in time. He then went back into the house, grabbed his jacket and house keys and joined her on the porch again.

"I want you to show me exactly where they were standing," he said. "I'll follow you in my car, but we'll have to hurry before we're drenched with rain."

CHAPTER FOURTEEN

By the time they got to the clearing by the river's edge, the clouds had turned the same color gray as Ava's tank top. Gabriel stood by the river and turned his back to the hilltop above.

"I'll be the mystery man, and you be Michelle," he said. "This is how you saw them standing?"

"Yes," Ava said, stepping forward. "She was very close to him, shouting in his face, and he was shouting back. That's the only way I was able to hear them above the water."

"What were they arguing about?"

"She was apologizing for her affair and you...I mean, whoever it was said she was destroying his career and that it was over between them."

"And then what?"

"Well, he said something else, she slapped him and then they kissed."

"Why didn't you tell me this before?"

"Because it was none of my business, and like I said, the man she was with looked a lot like you. Why would I tell you I saw you having an argument with your wife?"

He shook his head. "Michelle and I didn't argue. We ignored our problems. She also kept her emotions at bay and would never show how pissed she was at me by slapping me."

He paused and thought for a moment. "How did he kiss her?"

Ava shrugged. "What does that matter?"

"I'm telling you right now it wasn't me, but if you want to be sure, try to remember the way he kissed her. Is it the way I kiss you?"

Even though they were outside, the air suddenly felt suffocating. At the mention of kisses, she felt her breath begin to hitch as she thought about the way he'd hold her in his arms when his lips tasted hers and his tongue delved into her mouth to explore her to the point where he was coaxing moans from her.

"I don't know. I don't care. I didn't really stick around long enough to notice. As soon as it became intimate, I left. Then, I heard a scream and ran back, but by the time I got back to the hillside, they were gone."

He stayed silent but moved in close to her. Too close. She had to back away, but Gabriel continued to match her steps.

"What's wrong?" he asked.

"It's going to rain soon, and I've given you all the details I can remember from that day."

She started to turn away, but he turned her back around just as thunder sounded above them.

"Hang on a minute. You suddenly want to tell me about stuff that happened five years ago, so how about we go further back before all of this? Tell me why you got on a plane to Phoenix and ghosted me for eight months."

"No."

"You don't think I deserve an explanation?"

"You want an explanation? Here's one: "I told you the night you and your friends came into the bar that I wasn't good for you. I guess I had to show you for you to believe me."

The sky opened up and rain began to pelt down on them, dampening his hair and face and causing his green eyes to crystallize.

"Bullshit!" He shouted above the rain. "You know what I think? I think you're just too scared to be happy. You know how good you and I were together, but you just couldn't let that chip on your shoulder go, and you had to fuck everything up."

"And you know me so well," she said her voice dripping with sarcasm as she wiped her face and pushed her damp hair away from her eyes.

"You're damn right I do."

"You don't know a thing."

"You told me last night you didn't want to leave me."

"I know what I said."

"Did you mean it?"

"Yes, I meant it!"

"But you took $250,000 from him and ran off! Then you stayed gone for months—"

"And you got married."

"To a woman I never loved and who never loved me. And it's all because the woman I really wanted was a coward and would rather have money—"

"Because I was pregnant, and I was scared!"

He went completely silent and shock seemed to envelope him like a glove. "What?"

She wrapped her arms around her waist, trying to trap warmth inside her against the cold rain.

"I was pregnant. Your father may have been a jerk, but he was right. You were going places, and the last thing you needed was to be saddled with a child. I didn't mean to get pregnant, but it happened, and I knew I was going to need help."

He shook his head as if trying to clear his confusion. "Wait. You said you *were* pregnant."

"I lost the baby at eight weeks." She snorted with self-deprecation. "How's that for irony? I take money to help me care for our child and there ends up not being a child. I stayed gone, because I didn't know how to face you, and I was upset about the baby. Then, months later, Tess called me and told me you were married. I thought you were happy and that it was safe to come back to Gypsy Bay."

She looked around at the trees surrounding them, with their roots strong and withstanding the storm that was raging. She wished she was just as courageous to weather the storms in her own life. If she was, she would never have been standing here and telling him that five years ago, he was almost a father. Instead, on that fateful day, she would've ripped up that check in Paul Meyer's face and told Gabriel right then that they were going to be parents. Even if she still miscarried, at least she wouldn't have had to suffer through it without him.

"Seeing you married was really hard for me, so I did my best to avoid you, finished school and got a job at the sheriff's office. Then Michelle was killed, I was head of the investigation, and suddenly you were always there." She turned back to look at him. "I couldn't stop thinking about you. I had to leave."

CHAPTER FIFTEEN

*L*ightning struck and thunder boomed above them. Its reverberating roar seemed to awaken Gabriel from a daze. He took her by the arm and led her back to the lot where they parked their cars. At that point, he got in his car and she got in hers, and they each drove away without another word to each other.

At the intersection of Franklin Road, Gabriel went right in the direction of his home, and Ava went left. By the time she reached her house, the downpour had been elevated to an outright storm. She got out of the car, ran to her front door, let herself inside and then slammed it shut behind her. She then leaned against it, closing her eyes and imagined the shock that painted his face. She'd told him the truth, so why did it feel as if the invisible wall between them had been erected even higher?

Pushing herself away from the door, she dragged herself upstairs, removed her wet clothes and put on a dry cotton robe. She grabbed a towel from the bathroom and patted her damp hair. As she went back downstairs toward the kitchen to make some tea, her doorbell sounded. She turned to the front door, unlocked it and pulled it open. Gabriel stood on the threshold, soaking wet from rainwater.

"Gabriel," she said, eyes wide. "What are you doing? Come inside."

Without a word, he stepped inside and looked around her home as if he wasn't there just several hours ago.

"Are you all right?" she asked, shutting the door.

His eyes made another sweep around her living area, and he still hadn't said a word.

"Gabriel?"

Finally, he turned to look at her. "I'm sorry I bailed like that. I just didn't know what to say."

She nodded her understanding.

He wiped raindrops from his face. "If you hadn't miscarried, would you have ever told me?"

"I'm sure eventually I would've told you, but seeing as there was no baby, I didn't see any reason to burden you—"

"Stop," he said, slicing the air with one hand. "Burden me? Jesus, it's the same thing with you. You're still trying to scare me away, but from what? What should I be scared of?"

She hitched her shoulders. "Maybe I wasn't trying to scare you away. Maybe it was me who was scared."

His eyes slowly moved up and down her body and he didn't hesitate to close the short distance between them.

"Scared of what?" He asked, reaching out a hand and slowly slipping one side of her robe down and baring her right shoulder. "Of being with me?"

"Yes. You were right about what you said earlier. I was scared to be happy."

He bent low and kissed her shoulder. She shivered from his lips that were cold and wet from the rain, but felt so good against her warm skin.

"Being with you," she breathed. "It terrifies me."

He moved his lips from her shoulder to the inner curve of her neck and kissed there. "What about it terrifies you?"

"This," she said on a sigh and moan. "All of this."

He moved to the other side of her neck and planted his lips there. "What?"

"The way…how good you make me feel."

Gabriel slipped the rest of her robe down, exposing the left shoulder and even lower still until her breasts were uncovered. He caressed his fingers lightly down the center of her chest between her breasts and stared deeply into her eyes, his green orbs burning. He looked down at his own fingers trailing down her chest and over her breasts. He then looked up at her, watching as pleasure overcame her.

"I can't do this with you."

"Yes, you can."

"Gabriel—"

"Just let it happen."

He snaked his hand around her neck and brought his mouth down to meet her lips. Ava met his kiss with her own assault. She moaned into his mouth, but it ended as fast as it had begun when Gabriel pulled away, bent his head low and put his hot, searing mouth to her breasts.

Ava cried out from surprise at the pleasure that coursed through her. She pressed her fingers to the back of his head and brought him in closer, aching to feel every sensation of his tongue as it circled and teased her nipples. It felt unbelievable that Ava couldn't help her body as it developed a rhythm of its own. She rotated her hips, grinding into him to feel that hard, rigid part of him she was desperate for.

His mouth left her breasts to nip at one of her earlobes and whispered, "You want it here or upstairs?"

"Upstairs," she panted.

He put his hands to her waist, opening the robe wide enough until she was fully exposed to him. His hands went to her bare ass, gripped it and lifted her in the air. The feeling of her wet center flushed against the rigidness of his jeans made her gasp.

"Gabriel," she moaned and encircled her arms around his neck as he carried her up the stairs to her loft bedroom.

He practically tossed her on the soft duvet, and she lay there, hypnotized at the sight of him removing every item of his clothing. He kept his eyes on her, too, even when he was down to nothing and silently dared her to look away. But she kept her focus on him, all of him, and her heart raced with the anticipation of feeling him inside her after so many years.

His green eyes brightened with desire as he bent over her, slipped a hand between her thighs and hissed out a curse when he felt how wet she was. Ava's body rose off the bed in response to his touch, and her eyes trailed him as he bent his head low, further this time, to the center of her legs. He pushed her knees apart and bent lower still. Ava held her breath and continued to watched, mesmerized as his face disappeared between her thighs. The next sensation she felt was his tongue lapping her up with greed.

She jerked and cried out, unable to control herself. Her fingers gripped the pillows above her head, while his fingers gripped her thighs, keeping them spread and holding her in the position that gave him free access to her core. She begged for him over and over, while his tongue worked its magic and made her feverish. But as she felt that unmistakable, powerful wave coming over her, Gabriel sat up, planted his knees on the bed and hooked his arms underneath her legs. With one swift motion, he pulled her to the edge of the bed and entered her, pushing his way through her tightness and began stroking her tenderly.

She kept her hands above her head, allowing him to rock her body back and forth to a sensual rhythm while she moaned her desire for him. Gabriel leaned forward, brushed her hair from her face and kissed her long and deep.

"You're still mine," he whispered, locking his gaze on her and pushing himself deeper.

"Yes," she said, inhaling the scent of his aftershave mixed with rainwater.

His hands on her hips tightened as he quickened his strokes. "Say it."

The pressure built inside of her. "I'm still yours!"

"Good girl."

Those two words were enough to send her over the edge. She clawed at his back, locked her legs around him like a vice and held on as her orgasm came with the force of a tidal wave. She cried out for him, allowed him to take all of her until he finally bellowed his own pleasure and released deep inside of her.

CHAPTER SIXTEEN

The next morning, while Gabriel showered, Ava made coffee and grabbed his clothes from the dryer. She then made the bed, while wanting so much to crawl back into it with him, cuddle with him, maybe make love once more and then get up to make breakfast. It's what normal people did, but she and Gabriel were in an abnormal situation. They cared for each other, they missed each other, but their future? She wasn't sure what would become of them, especially now that she was in charge of Chris and Michelle's murder investigations.

Then there was the baby and the fact that she still chose to take a payout instead of being with him. Did he forgive her for leaving without talking to him? Could he ever forgive her?

"You're thinking too hard."

She heard his voice while at the same time he came up behind her and wrapped his arms around her waist. She dropped the throw pillow she'd been clutching and slowly turned in his arms to face him.

"Good morning," she greeted.

In return, he kissed her softly on the lips, and she realized he was still damp from his shower and wearing nothing but one of her towels around his waist.

"Everything all right?" he asked, moving to the curve of her neck.

She moaned in delight and simply nodded her head, succumbing to the sensation of his lips on her skin.

"What did I tell you about this robe," he murmured, still focused on her neck, but at the same time, moving his hands from her waist to undo the tie.

She smiled. "I was just about to get into the shower after you were done."

"Why didn't you join me?" he asked, and in seconds the knot was untied.

Ava grabbed her robe, before he exposed her naked body and stepped away from him.

"Not so fast. I have a witness to interview this morning. I got the voicemail from our receptionist, so I need to get going."

Disappointment shadowed his face, but he nodded. "It's all right. I have some appointments myself."

She started to walk away, but he held onto her wrist, stopping her and gently pulling her back.

"One thing first: I'm sorry for the way I reacted," he said. "You told me about the baby, and I didn't know what to say."

"It's all right."

"No, it's not. You shouldn't have had to deal with that alone in the first place. I pushed you to give me an explanation of why you left, and when you did, I just shut down."

She nodded, placed a hand on the side of his stubbled face and kissed him softly. She then gestured to the armchair in the corner of her bedroom.

"Your clothes are over there. I put them in the dryer last night after you fell asleep."

"Thank you."

They then lapsed into a silence she had been trying to avoid, that awkward silence when they were both wondering the same thing.

"So, what happens now?" Gabriel asked, obviously brave enough to voice his thoughts.

Before she could say she didn't have an answer for him, the doorbell rang. She tied her robe once more and stepped past him.

"I'll get it. There's coffee downstairs whenever you're ready."

She didn't wait for his reply, but closed the bedroom door and made her way downstairs to the front door. Whoever was on the other side knocked again with impatience.

"Just a minute," she called out and looked through her peephole.

When she saw who it was, her entire body stilled from surprise. It was only genuine curiosity that made her unbolt the locks and slowly open her door to the visitor.

"Mr. Meyer," she greeted. "What can I do for you?"

Paul Meyer stood on the other side of the threshold with another older man. Both were dressed in tailored suits and looking distinguished.

"Sorry to disturb you, Deputy Beckett, but I was looking for my son. I called his office and was told he hadn't checked in. Then I went to his home and he wasn't there either." He paused and looked over his shoulder toward the curb.

"That's his car, so I'm going to assume he's here with you."

There was so much she wanted to say to this man, but at the moment, all words failed her and only memories began to invade her thoughts to the point that she was just speechless.

"Dad?"

Paul and the other man looked over her shoulder, and

Ava turned to see Gabriel coming up behind her, now fully dressed and putting on his tie.

"What are you doing here?" Gabriel asked.

Paul's eyes narrowed in consternation. "I could ask you the same question, but I can already guess and—"

"And it's none of your business," Gabriel finished.

"You're giving a speech today at City Hall," Paul said.

"I'm aware of that. Did you think I needed an escort?"

Paul acknowledged him with concealed anger for just a moment longer and then gestured to his companion beside him.

"This is Walter Fallon. I hired him to help you refine some of the points in your speech. This is very important. The voters need to see your confidence and feel assured that you're the best man for the job."

Ava could feel Gabriel stiffen behind her. She could imagine there were a lot of words running through his mind that he wanted to tell his father, but out of respect for her and Walter Fallon, he decided not to showcase the family drama.

But Paul had apparently seen enough and could no longer contain his thoughts.

"Jesus, Gabriel, what are you doing?"

"Excuse me?"

Paul gestured around the quiet neighborhood. "What if someone was out walking their dog or just happened to drive by and see you coming out of the house of the woman who's investigating you for murder? A woman you had a relationship with years ago? It wouldn't take much to start the gossip mill running."

"Like I said, it's none of your business," Gabriel gritted.

"But it is my business. It's everyone's business, son, because you are running for public office. Everyone in this neighborhood is a potential voter!"

Paul must've realized he was raising his voice and attracting unwanted attention, because he visibly breathed in and out, but still regarded both Gabriel and Ava with malice.

"Give me a minute," Gabriel said, reaching past Ava and closing the door in his father's face.

Ava looked at the closed front door with surprise and then up at Gabriel, who also looked to be trying to calm himself.

"Are you all right?" she asked.

"Yeah, he just…" he sent a disgusted look toward the door as if his father could still see him and then shook his head.

"You should go," she said. "I didn't know you had a speech to make."

"That and a few other meetings, but I should be free by late afternoon." He paused. His temper slowly receded and his attention was now fully on her. "Do you want to have dinner?"

She absolutely wanted to, but there were still so many unanswered questions between them.

"Let's play it by ear," she said.

He frowned. "What's that supposed to mean?"

"It means, that Paul may need to work on his delivery, but he's right. I'm in the middle of an investigation involving you and your murdered wife. Don't you think we should resolve that before you and I start planning dates?"

He didn't say anything, but moved away from her and grabbed his jacket. He shrugged it on with angry movements, and by the time he looked at her again, his eyes had gone cold.

"Gabriel?"

"Once again, you're letting everyone else decide what happens between us."

"This is my job. Don't you want to find her killer?"

He grabbed for his keys off her console table and chuckled. "You know, the Sheriff asked me that same question, and I said yes, because that's what a man in my position is supposed to say. But if it keeps me away from you, maybe I don't want to find the killer. Maybe I don't care anymore. Maybe for so long, I pretended to be happy and in love with a woman who I only married, because her family name would be good for my career, and now I'm tired of pretending. I'm tired of all of it!"

He ran his hands through his hair in frustration. "When you came back, I started to think that maybe we had a second chance, but I shut it away, because I didn't want to get my hopes up and believe that you might actually want me, too. Then last night happened."

He stepped forward, grasping her face between his hands. "Tell me that was the beginning of our second chance."

"I don't know what it was," she said, truthfully. "All I can tell you is that I'll be here. When we finally get to talk about us, I'll be here."

"For how long?"

She backed away from him, feeling as if he'd just slapped her in the face with those words. "That's not fair."

His eyes roamed her face, but without another word, he turned away and opened the front door to a waiting Paul and Walter.

"Let's go," he said, and closed the door behind him with a loud bang.

CHAPTER SEVENTEEN

Mr. Lee sat in Ava's visitor's chair at her desk, clutching the cup of coffee she'd given him and gave his statement as best he could. Ava sat across from him with her pen poised over her notepad and listened intently as he recounted what he saw five years ago.

"My wife and I went to one of Commissioner Lacey's rallies. She was so excited to meet him and started talking about how we were almost involved in a murder." He shook his head in regret. "That's how I got your name."

"Commissioner Lacey said you had some information about the murders from that night," she clarified.

"You have to understand I never heard about the murders," Mr. Lee said. "My family and I live in Salt Lake City, and we visit Gypsy Bay once in a while for vacation. That's why I never came forward. If I'd known what happened…"

"It's all right, Mr. Lee," Ava said, trying to sound calm and assuring, despite her excitement. He was the first eyewitness in this case, and she was on pins and needles waiting to hear his account. "Just tell me what you saw that night."

He took a deep breath. "It was at the Hideaway River cabins. It was our last night in Gypsy Bay, and I'd ordered a couple of pizzas for the family and stepped outside to wait for the delivery guy. While I waited, I scrolled through my phone for a bit until I heard a car pull up."

"Go on," Ava prompted.

"I thought it was the pizza guy, so I looked up, but there was no pizza sign on his car, and he hadn't stopped in front of my cabin. He'd pulled up to another cabin and just sat there with the engine running. I thought it was another guest, so I went back to looking through my phone."

He paused to take a sip of his coffee. "Well, nothing happened for a while, but then I heard the car door open, and I looked up to see the man get out. He was wearing dark blue jeans and a navy-blue hooded sweatshirt. I wouldn't have thought anything of it, but he was moving away from his car, and I saw that the engine was still running."

"What did you do then?"

He shrugged. "I nearly called out to him to tell him he left his car running, but he walked up to the cabin door and just stood there."

"Do you know which cabin number he was standing in front of?"

"Number five. Just three doors down from mine."

"And you say he just stood there?"

"That's right. It looked like he couldn't decide whether to go inside or not. I finally called out to him. I said, 'You okay sir?', and he whipped around as if I'd startled him. That's when I got a clear look at him. He didn't say anything, but raised the hood of his sweatshirt over his head, got back in his car and drove off."

Ava nodded, jotting down everything as fast as she could. "And you say you recognized this person?"

"That's right. We left Gypsy Bay the next morning, and I

had no idea what had happened in that cabin. It's kind of creepy knowing my family was only staying a few yards from a murder scene. Anyway, my wife and I were having lunch in town just yesterday, and I saw him as he passed by the restaurant. I instantly remembered him from that night. Then we heard a couple in the booth across from us mention that his wife had been murdered in those cabins five years ago."

Ava's hand froze in midair over the notepad. She looked up at Mr. Lee in disbelief.

"Well, that just floored me," he continued, seemingly unaware of the disturbance he'd just caused. "I realized then I had better get in contact with the authorities and tell them what I knew. My wife, on the other hand, finds the whole thing exciting."

Ava cleared her throat. "His wife?"

Mr. Lee's eyebrows rose in question. "What was that?"

"Um, you said the man you saw…it was his wife that had been murdered in the cabins?"

"That's right."

Jesus, it can't be true. "You're telling me that night, the night Chris Foster and Michelle Meyer were killed, you saw—"

"Her husband," Mr. Lee finished. "Gabriel Meyer."

CHAPTER EIGHTEEN

The crowd gave a raucous cheer and applause as Gabriel's speech came to an end. He smiled as the cameras flashed and came forward to clasp the hands of his supporters and potential voters. He stepped down from the podium, and the crowd surged forward as several people angled for his attention.

"Mr. Meyer! Mr. Meyer!" Diana pushed her way through the crowd and rushed up to him.

"What is it, Diana?" he asked, still smiling and shaking hands.

She came close to him and whispered in his ear. "There are some deputies here, and they want to speak with you."

Gabriel frowned then looked past her to see that there were indeed a group of deputies making their way toward him. Diana ushered Gabriel to the side, away from the crowd, and he addressed the uniformed officers.

"What can I do for you, gentlemen?"

"Mr. Meyer, we have orders to escort you to the sheriff's office for questioning. You have the right to have an attorney present."

"I have the right to an attorney? Are you arresting me?"

"We'd prefer to not do that out here in the open as a courtesy to you. If you would just follow us down to the station."

Paul Meyer fought his way through the crowd and stepped up to them. "What's going on here?"

"Dad, let me handle this," Gabriel said and then turned back to the deputies. "Where's Deputy Beckett?"

"She's at the station now, waiting for you," one of them replied.

He nodded. "All right. Let's go."

They escorted him to an SUV and open the door for him to get inside.

"Gabriel, I'm sending my attorney over straight away," Paul said, just as the doors to the SUV closed.

During the short drive to the sheriff's station, Gabriel tried not to think about why he was being brought in, but somewhere in the recesses of his mind, he knew that his secret had been found out.

When they arrived at the station, he was escorted into a private room and for several moments, he was alone. Gabriel didn't sit down, but took off his suit jacket and paced the floor with impatience. Finally, the door opened and the woman he'd spent the night making love to walked in wearing an unreadable expression.

"What the hell's going on?" he asked.

"Take a seat, Mr. Meyer."

"Mr. Meyer?" he echoed, sarcastically. "Ava, what's going on?"

She slapped a folder on the table and stared across from him with firm brown eyes. "What's going on is I'm conducting an interview, and I need you to take a seat."

He challenged her stare for several tense moments and then finally pulled out a chair and sat down. She did the same, opposite from him and opened the file.

"Did the deputies inform you of your rights?"

"Just ask your questions," he said, coldly.

Her eyes trailed over him briefly and then she launched into her first question that confirmed his earlier fears.

"Why did you go to the Hideaway River cabins the night of Michelle's and Chris's deaths?"

"I didn't kill them."

Ava peered into his eyes, and he saw anger mixed with pain. "Answer the question."

"I knew Michelle was up to something. I'd known for a few months, and was willing to let it go, but I guess I didn't want to let it go anymore. I lied when I told her I had a full schedule. I cleared my schedule and instead borrowed a friend's car and followed her around that day until she came to the cabins."

Ava looked pained. "What were you hoping to accomplish?"

"I was going to confront them and tell Michelle that I was done and that I would be filing for divorce in the morning. I saw Chris go in and figured he was the man she was seeing behind my back. I got out of the car, walked up to the door, but I hesitated."

"Why?"

"I don't know. I guess I figured to myself what was the point. I wasn't in love with her. In fact, it was a relief to have visual proof that the marriage was over."

"A witness saw you outside the cabins."

He nodded. "I know. That's another reason why I left. I didn't know if he was a local or not, and there had already been enough town gossip spread about our marriage. I just went home and decided to wait until she finally came back to tell her it was over between us. But she never did come back." He raised his hands in surrender. "I thought the two of them had run away. I never thought in a million years they'd been killed."

"Why didn't you say anything to me or any of the deputies when we questioned you five years ago?"

"Because I knew how it would look. I followed my wife and her lover to the cabins, and people would think I went there in a jealous rage, but I didn't."

"Who cares what people would've thought? I'm in charge of this investigation, and I need to know everything. So why didn't you tell me, and don't give me that bullshit about it making you look suspicious. The witness didn't see you go inside, but there's a back door to that cabin—"

"Ava—"

"So, you keeping quiet all this time, makes me wonder if you decided to find another way in to kill your wife and her lover!"

She was visibly shaking from anger, and instead of defending himself, he wanted more to take her hand and clutch it in his own. She didn't really believe he could be a murderer, did she?

"Look at me," he said. "You know I didn't do this. I'm sorry for keeping silent. It's not the first time I've done something stupid, but it doesn't make me guilty. We may have been apart for five years, but you still know me."

"All I've asked from the beginning is for you to be honest and upfront with me."

He felt his temper rising again. He was on the defensive, and he didn't like it one bit. "You mean how honest and upfront you were about the baby?"

They were staring at each other with warring eyes, until the door opened, startling them both. Gray stood there, his broad and muscled frame filling the doorway and dividing a look between him and Ava.

"Deputy Beckett, may I have a word with you?"

"I'm in the middle of an interview, sir."

"The interview is over," Gray said. "Mr. Meyer's attorney has just arrived, and I need to speak with you. Now."

Gabriel rose to his feet. "I didn't ask to see a lawyer. Let her continue the interview." He was desperate to get her to believe that he had nothing to do with this. He needed to erase that uncertainty and doubt from her eyes.

"Gabe, stay out of this," Gray ordered. "Sit down and wait for your lawyer. Deputy Beckett, come with me."

CHAPTER NINETEEN

"Paul Meyer is a prick," Gray began as soon as Ava entered his office.

She started to sit down, but paused in surprise at the use of his language.

"I never liked him, especially since he's made it his personal hobby to try to rally his colleagues to vote against me in every election. So, imagine how it feels to have that prick march his self-righteous ass into my office, demanding that my newest deputy be removed from the Meyer-Foster case, because and I quote: 'She has developed an unprofessional relationship with the widower.'"

Ava sat down in the chair and slowly closed her eyes from embarrassment. "I made a mistake."

"Were you ever going to tell me?" Gray asked.

"You would've taken me off the case."

"You're damn right. What choice have you left me?"

"Sheriff, if you could just give me some more time. I feel like I'm close to something."

"What? The murderer? You really want to go back in

there and pin a murder on a man you just slept with last night?"

"No, not Gabriel. I—I don't know."

Gray eyed her with sympathy, then rubbed his face and sighed aloud. "I'm sorry, Ava. You've done great work so far, but I'm taking you off this case and reassigning you, effective immediately."

* * *

"So, I would say a lot has happened since I last saw you," Tess said, flipping through the channels until she settled on a news station.

Neither of them was really paying attention to the anchor crew. It was mainly for white noise as Ava retold the events of that day beginning with the fact that she woke up, lying next to Gabriel.

"I knew this would happen," Ava said, tucking her feet underneath her in the large armchair of Tess's sitting area. The room was spacious enough to accommodate guests of her bed and breakfast, but this was the slow travel season in Gypsy Bay, so they had the room to themselves.

"I never should've gone there with him."

"Don't start feeling sorry for yourself," Tess scolded. "You're human, and the two of you have a volatile, unresolved history with the investigation, the payoff and your unborn baby."

"Exactly! We should be sitting and talking about those things, not falling into bed with one another."

"Well, then it's obvious the attraction you have for each other is much stronger than you think."

Ava sighed. "Stop making excuses for me. I messed up, and now I'm off the case. But I guess it's for the best. Hell, before Sheriff Spencer came into the interview room, I was this close to accusing my ex-boyfriend of murdering his wife."

"Seriously? Gabriel?"

"I don't have proof, but there's a lot he hid from me about that night."

They fell into companionable silence and Ava turned her head to stare at the television as mainly a way to distract her from thinking about the downward spiral her life had become.

On screen was a replay of Jake Lacey giving his speech in front of City Hall. Ava remembered the day she drove by, while he was giving the speech for his campaign. The camera focused in on Jake as he smiled brilliantly for the voters and then he looked to his wife and outstretched his hand as a gesture for her to come forward. When she was within inches of him, he pulled her into him and kissed her. The crowd loved it.

"That's sweet," Tess said, sharing the same sentiment as the crowd.

But Ava was frowning. She untucked her legs from underneath her and sat forward in the chair, getting closer to the television and watching the couple's loving embrace.

"What is it?" Tess asked.

"There's something..." she began. "I thought I saw..."

Try to remember the way he kissed her. Is it the way I kiss you?

Gabriel's words struck her like a bolt of lightning, bringing with them realization and the truth. Ava stood in an instant.

"What's the matter," Tess asked, startled. "Jesus, Ava, you look as if you've seen a ghost."

"That's exactly what I did see."

"Okay, you're scaring me." Tess slowly rose from her chair and went to stand by Ava. She looked to the television screen trying to see what Ava saw, but by now, the news anchor had moved onto another segment. But Ava was still seeing it unravel in her mind and recalling more snatches of conversation.

Everyone in this town knows you jog that trail in the mornings. Everyone knows your routine.

"Ava?"

She grabbed her purse and car keys and dashed toward the front door. "I have to go. I'll call you later."

"Wait, where are you going?"

She could hear Tess calling after her, but she didn't have time to explain. She couldn't even make sense of it herself right now and had to get somewhere quiet where she could sort it all out.

"Ava," Tess called. "Ava, just tell me what you saw."

She opened the front door, paused and turned back around to her best friend. "I saw a kiss."

CHAPTER TWENTY

"Deputy Beckett, to what do I owe the pleasure?" Jake Lacey asked, as he gestured for Ava to have a seat. "Can I get you a drink?"

"Nothing for me," she said, continuing to stand. "I wanted to thank you for sending Mr. Lee to me. He's a very helpful witness."

Jake blushed. "I'll be honest with you. He and his wife told me he saw Gabriel before I gave you his number. I didn't want to say anything until you spoke to him directly. Is it true?"

"Yes, I interviewed Mr. Meyer, and he confirmed he was at the cabins that night."

Jake shook his head. "He needs to just confess to it all and let this town rest—especially Carmen. This can't be easy for her."

"That's what I wanted to talk to you about, Mr. Lacey." Ava brushed her hand across a wooden table stand that held a vase of lilies.

"Why are you so certain the murderer is Gabriel Meyer?"

He looked sheepish. "I don't want to tell you how to do

your job, but it's kind of obvious. Michelle was due to come into money, but I don't think Gabriel cares too much about that. He has his own family money. But he is a proud man." He paused to look at her. "As I'm sure you know more than anyone."

Ava dodged that assumption. "Go on."

"Well, he's proud to a fault. He couldn't bear Michelle making a fool of him, and he could only take the rumors for so long."

"That's quite a theory, but I guess it would be beneficial to you if he was arrested," she said with a wink. "No more competition."

Jake frowned. "True, but I'm looking for justice, not votes."

"Of course. Speaking of which, I finally caught one of your speeches on television, and I have to say the interaction between you and Mrs. Lacey is very heartwarming."

He smiled. "My campaign manager said we should embrace after every speech I do, and show an American family in love and united. The voters love it."

"Yes, I can see that. It's almost as if you two are having a private moment." She paused and was sure to keep her eyes focused on his every movement. "Just like that day in the woods."

He reached for a carafe of whiskey and a glass, and she saw it—the slightest tremor in his hand. If she hadn't been looking, she would have missed it, because by the time he poured himself a drink and turned to face her, his cool and composed disguise had returned.

"Come again?"

Ava let a beat pass. "You were right about me knowing Gabriel. Some things about him, I can find similar in other men, things that can be imitated like height and body type and even the way he dresses. But there are certain things that can't be faked."

He shrugged with indifference. "Like what?"

"Mannerisms."

"I don't understand."

"A week before Michelle was killed, I was in Strawberry Woods, and I stood on the hillside and saw two people arguing in the clearing by the river. Two people who I thought at the time were Gabriel and Michelle Meyer."

Jake took a sip from his drink. "It wasn't?"

She shook her head slowly. "Nope. I was fooled. It was a completely different couple. A couple who knew how to behave in front of an audience. A couple who knew I'd be there, because of my jogging routine. This couple staged a scene and both disguised themselves to look like someone else."

He chuckled and shook his head, appearing confused. "You lost me."

"Then I'll make it plain. It was you and your wife there in the woods, pretending to be Gabriel and Michelle."

Jake froze. "You can't be serious."

She let her silence speak for her.

"That's insane! Why would Samantha and I ever impersonate Gabriel and Michelle?"

"To set up a frame. You already planned to kill Michelle and was setting up Gabriel to take the fall."

"Why would I kill Michelle?"

"Because she was no longer satisfied with being the other woman. She wanted to take the place of Samantha and be by your side. Michelle was *your* lover, not Chris Foster's, and as a rising political star, the last thing you wanted was your mistress out of control."

Jake put his glass of whiskey down on the table. "I don't

know where you're getting all these ideas, but I think it's time you leave."

"I saw the way you kissed your wife on TV. It was the exact way you embraced her there in the woods. It's very difficult to imitate natural affection, especially if you've never seen Gabriel embrace Michelle."

"Deputy Beckett, I'm asking you to leave."

"How did you know that stone belonged to me?"

"What?"

She pulled the necklace with the lapis lazuli gem on it from her pocket and showed it to him. "How did you know this belonged to me? How did you find it?"

He shrugged with annoyance. "It was on the trail. It must've fallen off while you were running."

She shook her head slowly again. "It came off when I fell down the hillside. You could've only found it on the side or down at the bottom of the hill, and the only two people who would know where to look for it was the person that fell and the one who pushed them."

He rounded his desk and picked up the phone. "I'm calling security to escort you out."

"Don't bother, honey."

They both turned toward the door and saw that Samantha had soundlessly entered the office, holding a gun. Ava immediately went for her side arm, but Samantha aimed the gun at her heart.

"I wouldn't, Deputy Beckett. I've always liked you and don't want to shoot you."

"Sam, put it down," Jake said. His annoyance was gone and now a tinge of panic sounded in his tone. "You don't need to do this. Let me call our lawyer. She has no proof of anything she's saying."

"But she knows! And that's all it takes." Samantha kept her eyes and the gun trained on Ava. "I heard about your reputation in L.A. You're very smart. Yes, we can deny it and maybe you don't have proof, but you'll never let this go, and I don't want to sit around and wait for you to one day arrest us both on the campaign trail."

She sent a sly smile towards Ava. "I was listening at the door, and wow! That was very clever of you to figure out our little romantic scene. Jake and Gabriel are about the same height and build, but I had him cut his hair short to match and bought him the same dark gray pullover and baseball cap I've seen Gabriel wear. For myself, I just bought a wig to match Michelle's hair color, put on some sunglasses because it was sunny and voila!"

"Then you screamed," Ava said.

"That was for added effect. I saw over Jake's shoulder that you left, so I screamed, hoping you'd come back and think something awful happened, thus planting suspicion for Gabriel in your mind."

She smiled, looking very pleased with her plan. "By all accounts, it worked, but who knew that something so simple as a kiss would give us away?"

"Please, put the gun down," Jake said.

Jake was, unknowingly, distracting his wife each time he pled with her to drop the gun, and each time she turned his way, Ava came a few inches closer. She just needed to get within arm's reach of that gun.

* * *

Gabriel drove aimlessly through town, avoiding going home, because home is where it was silent and silence brought on thoughts of Ava. He knew now it would've been better for him to just come clean to her about following Michelle that night, but how could it even cross her mind that he would hurt anyone?

He drove through the downtown streets thinking maybe he'd stop somewhere and have dinner, since for the first time, he decided to not join his father for their weekly meal. His father had been texting and calling him non-stop, wondering where he was, but Gabriel knew he couldn't sit through another prime rib meal and not lose his temper. Yes, he wanted Ava off the case to keep her out of danger, but his father had made the call to the Sheriff out of spite and told him what happened between her and Gabriel, which could put her career in jeopardy. He'd gone too far and Gabriel was fed up with the constant interference in his life.

As he drove by City Hall, he noticed the offices of Jake Lacey and slowed down. The man hadn't stopped his attempts to recruit Gabriel to become part of his team. Gabriel had refused meeting after meeting with him, because he knew what the purpose would be. He wasn't dropping out of the election for anyone, especially for a man who feared the competition. Gabriel pulled into a parking space in front of the offices and shut off his engine. With the day he had with Ava and his father, he was in the perfect mood to tell Jake to his face to give it up.

* * *

"Sam—" Jake started.

"This is the only way! If you're squeamish, leave the room. I'll take care of everything. Just like I took care of Michelle."

"But this isn't the way. If you just let me handle this—"

"Are you serious? You can't even handle one mistress! You came whining to me about her, and I came up with the plan to get rid of her. I take care of everything for you: the campaign, the voters, the staff, and even your little whores."

At those last words, Samantha took her eyes off Ava and looked at her husband. The hurt and betrayal she felt could clearly be seen. But as Ava made her final steps within reach of Samantha, the office door flew open.

It swung into Samantha's back, making her stumble forward, but she rapidly regained her balance and turned her gun toward the door and fired. That half-second distraction was all Ava needed. She pulled her gun from her side holster and fired without hesitation. The bullet struck Samantha in the shoulder and the impact had her careening against the wall.

"Sam!"

"Stay right there, Lacey," Ava commanded as she stepped over to Samantha where she lay on the floor panting heavily.

She kicked the gun out of the woman's hand and then trained her own pistol on Jake Lacey who stood motionless and afraid for his wife. She sensed movement to her left and tossed one brief look that way to see Gabriel standing in the doorway. Relief swept through her.

"The door was still open," he said, breathing heavily from adrenaline. "I didn't know what else to do, and hoped it would distract her."

"Are you hit?" she asked.

"No, I stepped out of the way in time."

Ava nodded. "I need you to call the sheriff's office."

"Already done." Gabriel stepped fully into the room and when he saw Samantha on the floor, he shrugged off his jacket, knelt down beside her and pressed it to her wound. She cried out in pain, but he kept pressure on it.

"I heard the commotion from the hall and called from my cell phone," he said.

She shook her head with irritation, but didn't take her eyes off Jake. "You should have stayed out there. You could've been hurt."

"Fuck that. I wasn't going to leave you alone in here with these two."

She wanted to argue, but she couldn't deny that his timing had been perfect. Then her anxiety began to lessen as she heard the sound of police sirens blaring down the street. While they waited for her colleagues, Ava read both Jake and Samantha Lacey their Miranda rights.

CHAPTER TWENTY-ONE

"Whenever you're ready, Commissioner," Gray said, switching on the recorder.

Ava, Sheriff Gray Spencer, Jake Lacey and his lawyer all sat at a square metal card table in the same interview room Ava had questioned Gabriel earlier that afternoon. Now, several hours had passed, and she'd gone from fearing a man she loved would become her main suspect, to having the killer and his accomplice in her sights.

Samantha Lacey had been taken directly to Gypsy Bay Memorial where she was being treated for the gunshot wound to her shoulder. After which, she would be handcuffed to her hospital bed until she was well enough to be taken into custody for two charges of conspiracy to commit murder.

"Chris Foster was blackmailing Michelle," Jake began. "He found out about the two of us and wanted money in exchange for his silence. Of course, the last thing I needed was for our affair to go public. Michelle told me about it and told me she would handle Chris and give him whatever he wanted, but I knew blackmailers like Chris would never go away. He would always want more. I exploded and told her it was over. That's when she threatened to tell Samantha everything."

"But Samantha already knew," Ava surmised.

Jake turned to her and nodded his head. "Yeah. My wife and I have an understanding. She allowed the occasional mistress as long as they stayed in line and didn't get their hopes up that they would one day take her place. Michelle… well, she wouldn't stay in line."

"I apologized for what I said and got her to calm down. But, I knew she was just a ticking time bomb and liable to go off at any moment. I guess I decided then that I needed to get rid of her. That's when Sam stepped in. She came up with the idea to first pretend to be Gabriel and Michelle, and act out an argument in the time and place where Deputy Beckett ran. Chris and Michelle would be killed and suspicion would be put on Gabriel."

"Take us through the night of the murder," Gray said.

Jake breathed in and out. His lawyer vehemently objected to him saying anything, but Ava could tell the man just wanted it all to end. It had been five years of him lying and covering up his crimes, and she guessed that in his confession, he finally felt free.

"I gave Michelle the idea to visit her trust lawyer to get the money for Chris. She told me he would never give it to her, but I convinced her to try. I just wanted it to look like she was getting money to run away with Chris. Of course, she wasn't able to get the money, so I took it from my campaign fund and gave it to her. She then told me the time and place she would meet Chris to give it to him. I told her I didn't want her meeting him alone and followed her to the Hideaway River cabins."

"Where was Samantha?" Ava asked.

"Hidden in the backseat. I didn't want Michelle to see her and suspect something was up."

She nodded for him to continue.

He sighed heavily. "I parked my car in the rear of the cabins, nestled in the trees and waited. When she sent me a text that he was there, I got out of my car, walked up to the back cabin door and knocked. She let me in, and just as Chris saw me, I shot him three times."

He paused and seemed to be gathering his strength. "I turned the gun on Michelle, but the way she looked at me, I almost didn't go through with it. Then she opened her mouth to scream, and I knew I had no choice. I shot her twice in the chest. I sent Samantha a text that it was done, she came in, and we staged their bodies to make it look as if they were lovers. Before we left, I grabbed the money, went to peek out the front window and jumped back when I saw Gabriel standing by the door."

"You saw Gabriel?" Ava asked.

He nodded. "It scared the shit out of me. He was just standing there, and it looked like he couldn't decide if he wanted to come in or not, but I could tell he hadn't seen me. Sam and I moved silently to the back door and left the way we came. We were nervous at first, but knew that him being there would make him look even more guilty."

"What did you do with the money?" Gray asked.

Jake looked to him and shrugged sheepishly. "I had my manager put it back in my campaign fund as an anonymous donor."

Gray looked to Ava, silently asking her if she had any more questions. Ava subtly shook her head, and Gray rose from his seat and escorted Jake and his lawyer to the holding cells where he would await trial.

When Ava came out of the interview room, she noticed Gabriel and Carmen standing there. Carmen's face was flushed red and tears streamed down her face. They had both been listening in another room.

Ava stepped up to her. "That's all for now, Mrs. Foster. If we need anything further from you, we'll give you a call."

Carmen nodded and grasped Ava's hand. "Thank you for finally bringing this all to rest." Then she laughed softly. "I really don't know what's worse: Believing all these years he was a cheater or finding out he was a blackmailer."

Ava squeezed her hand gently and nodded in sympathy. Carmen then turned to Gabriel and hugged him. They were like soldiers who'd gone through battle together. Gabriel returned the hug and kissed her on the cheek before letting her go.

"You take care of yourself," he said.

"You too," Carmen replied and left the station.

Ava then turned to Gabriel. "Thank you, for saving my life."

He nodded. "Thank you for finding Michelle's killer. I called her parents while you were interviewing Jake. They send their gratitude and will probably be making a call to you themselves."

He tucked his hands in his pockets, looked down and then slowly rose his head again. "I have one question."

"Just one?" she asked, wryly.

A small smile creased his lips. "Before the Sheriff went into the interview room, he told me you put it all together from a kiss. I'm guessing it was the kiss you saw in the woods. The one you told me about?"

"That's right. You asked me the other day how he kissed her, and I blew it off, pretending I hadn't noticed."

"But you did. You watched them."

"Yes. I watched, thinking it was you and Michelle, and I..." she stopped herself, feeling foolish. "Forget it."

He came one step closer to her. "And instinct told you

that it wasn't me. I never held you that way. I never kissed you that way."

"Yeah, and if only I'd gone with that instinct, but…Jesus Christ…I was jealous!" She erupted, angry with herself at being conquered by a simple human emotion. "I was blinded by fucking jealousy, and I buried my own instincts."

They fell silent at her revelation. Gabriel made another move toward her, but before he could speak, his cell began to ring. He groaned, fished his phone from his pocket, frowned at the display and answered the call.

"Hello?"

Ava watched his features turn from curious to concerned and finally fearful.

"What's wrong?" she asked.

"Is he stable?" he asked the caller.

A beat passed and then he nodded frantically. "I'll be right there."

As soon as he ended the call, he grabbed his jacket from a nearby visitor's chair and turned to leave. "I have to go. My father just had a stroke."

CHAPTER TWENTY-TWO

Gabriel battled the mixed feelings inside of him while he watched his father resting in the hospital bed.

"The doctors said it was mild," Paul said, his voice raspy. "I was fortunate that it wasn't so severe to impair my speech."

"Yes, you are," Gabriel confirmed. "Can I get you anything?"

Paul shook his head. "I heard Jake Lacey and his wife were arrested."

Gabriel nodded. "He confessed to the murders. He was Michelle's lover, not Chris Foster. Ava solved it."

"Yes, I heard that, too."

"Yeah, despite your attempts to thwart her efforts by interfering in my life…" Gabriel stopped himself and shook his head with self-deprecation.

"What?" Paul asked.

"Nothing. I'm sorry. I don't know why I said that when I should be grateful that you're okay."

"Don't apologize. Good health or not, I deserve it. I was wrong about Ava."

"Dad, forget it, all right?"

"She was just doing her job, and I had no right to interfere —just like I had no right five years ago."

"What are you doing?" Gabriel asked. "Is this your attempt to get things off your chest, because of the stroke?"

"No, it's not about that."

"Good, because despite this setback, you're as strong as an ox. The doctor said it was mild, and that you're going to be fine."

"Will you just listen to me, please? I need to say something. Something I should've told you a long time ago."

Gabriel sighed and turned to pour his father a cup of water from the pitcher. "What is it?"

"I know you're still in love her."

Gabriel paused slightly and then continued pouring the water, before handing the cup to Paul.

"I may have once, but that was years ago. A lot has changed."

Paul grasped the cup between his hands and eyed Gabriel with a knowing look. "Considering I found you at her home, things haven't changed that much."

Gabriel shook his head and shrugged. "So, what of it?"

Silence hung in the air for a while before Paul spoke again.

"I owe you an apology, son. I owe both of you an apology. "It was never my place to offer her that money. If I hadn't, none of this would've happened. I see what it's done to our relationship, and I regret that most of all."

"No, if she hadn't cashed that check and ran away without telling me I was going to be a father, this wouldn't be happening."

"I knew she was pregnant, Gabriel."

"What?"

"It's why I offered her the money in the first place, and I'll be sorry for that for the rest of my days."

Gabriel moved to the foot of the bed, leaned forward and braced his hands on the railing. He lowered his head and tried to assimilate what was being revealed to him.

"I thought I was doing what was best for you, and all I did was mess things up." He sighed. "And there's something else you need to know. Something that might help the two of you come together again."

Gabriel slowly raised his head and looked at his father with questioning eyes.

CHAPTER TWENTY-THREE

November

As Gabriel moved through the crowd of supporters, shaking hands, and accepting congratulations, he realized he never needed the influence of a family name to ensure his victory. After Michelle's death, her family was too overcome with grief to influence his political career, and Gabriel didn't press them at all. Instead, he relied on his experience and his determination to give him a win.

A pang of regret stabbed his heart. If he had realized this a long time ago, he would've gone after Ava in Phoenix, L.A. or wherever else she decided to run away to, and brought her back here to Gypsy Bay to stand by his side.

He turned around when he felt a hand slap his back with warmth.

"Congratulations, son. I'm proud of you."

Gabriel clasped his father's hand a moment longer than usual. They'd had a rocky relationship, but he still appreciated him for being there and was thankful he was still in good health.

"Thanks, Dad."

Paul looked around the crowd gathered in the grand hall he'd rented for the celebration and looked very pleased with himself.

"You have a lot of support here. Even if Lacey hadn't withdrawn his bid, I would never have bet against you. You're what this town needs."

Gabriel nodded in silent gratitude and noticed his father's eyes slowly move from his and focus on a spot just beyond his shoulder.

"And here comes one of your biggest supporters of all."

He knew who his dad was talking about. At least, he fervently prayed it was who he was talking about. They'd barely spoken to each other in weeks, and he would hardly consider those conversations. They were short and stilted, and whenever he broached the topic of the two of them, she stopped him with the excuse that she had a case to wrap up and he had an election to focus on. So, in short, he missed the absolute fuck out of her. So much in fact, that he hesitated to turn around in fear of being disappointed that it wasn't her.

Then she spoke to him, and he couldn't help but look into her eyes.

"Hello, Commissioner Meyer."

He turned and saw Ava dressed in a form-fitting satin black suit with a knee-length skirt, blazer and black peep-toe shoes. Underneath the blazer a hint of lace peeked out, accentuating her cleavage and making him groan inwardly with desire. But what he loved most of all was her hair and the way she had it loosely clasped at the nape of her neck, yet leaving a few strands of wavy tendrils to frame her glowing face.

"It's good to see you, Ava," he greeted with exaggerated politeness.

"You too," she said, with a shy smile. She then looked past him to Paul. "I'm glad to see you on your feet, Mr. Meyer."

"Thank you, dear. You look beautiful this evening."

She nodded in appreciation and focused again on Gabriel, which made his breath hitch.

"Can I speak to you somewhere privately?"

"We can go upstairs to my office."

He led her to the elevator and they rode it in silence to the fourth floor where Gabriel's office was located. He unlocked the door and allowed her to enter before him. He then gestured for his private office in the back and Ava stepped inside.

"Have a seat," he said. "You want a drink?"

"No, thank you. I wanted to first tell you congratulations on your victory."

He took off his suit jacket and laid it across a chair. "It's not that hard when my opponent is awaiting trial for murder."

She cocked her head to one side and sent him a wry smile. "No, I guess not, but don't sell yourself short. This town loves you."

He eyed her hard. "Does this town include you?"

He noticed she hadn't sat down, but stood in the middle of the room clutching the small purse that matched her outfit. She was looking nervous and unsure of herself, and in all his years of knowing Ava, even back to high school, she'd been neither nervous nor unsure of anything.

"I also came here to apologize for what happened in our interview. I shouldn't have implied…"

"Implied what? That I murdered my wife and the man I thought was her lover?" Gabriel asked, finishing her thought.

"Are you going to let me apologize or are you going to just interrupt me?"

"I don't want or need any apologies from you. In fact, I don't want to talk about Michelle, Chris, Jake or anything about that case. It's closed. It's over." He moved in closer to her. "And it was all just a distraction from the real issue here."

Ava backed away from him. "What issue?"

"You and me." He continued to track her steps until she was backed against a wall and he had her completely cornered. "That's why you're really here, right?"

"I told you why I came here—to offer my congratulations and apologize for my suspicions."

"And then what?"

"What do you mean?"

"I mean when do we talk about us? When do we figure out what this is between us? That night at your house, was that just you missing my touch or was it something more?"

She tried to look away, but he grasped her chin and angled her face until she was once again looking up at him.

"Tell me what's going on."

She opened and closed her mouth several times before speaking. "It—it was something more. For a long time, I believed I wasn't good enough for you. Part of the reason I came back here was to tell you that I had been a coward. I should've fought harder for us. I should've realized then that not only were you good for me, but I was good for you, too."

He nodded. "That's a good start." He slowly looked down at her full cleavage pressed against his chest. "My dad was right about something after all."

"What's that?"

"You look beautiful tonight, but with that outfit, I'd say sexy was a better description."

"Thank you."

"To tell you the truth, I was hoping to get you alone, so I could take a peek at whatever this lacy material is underneath this blazer."

She didn't say a word, but her silence and the spark in her coffee brown eyes urged him on. He held her gaze as he lowered one hand and undid the button of her blazer with one snap and slowly parted the satin fabric. He then slid his eyes downward and took in the black lace corset that pushed her already full breasts together making them look delectable and tempting beyond belief. By the time he refocused his gaze on her, he was done talking.

He took her by the hand and led her to the sofa. He sat down and grasped her hands, looking up at her. Their gazes locked as she stepped between his legs and removed her jacket. Her eyes still didn't waver as she slowly and deliberately shimmied her black skirt up her legs and over her thick and delicious-looking brown thighs, bringing his fantasies to life. He held his breath as she spread her legs apart slightly and straddled his lap. Gabriel held her by the waist with one hand and released himself from his slacks with the other. He then reached up between her legs and pulled her panties to the side. Almost immediately, Ava rose up and slid down on him, and he hissed at the feel of her tightness caressing every inch of him.

"Jesus Christ," he uttered and proceeded to bounce her pretty ass up and down on his hardness, slowly at first and then increasing the pace.

"Gabriel," she cried out, welcoming each stroke.

He reached behind her and unclasped the barrette she wore in her hair. In seconds, her dark brown waves were flowing freely and covering them both like a curtain as she kissed him and moaned indecipherable words into his mouth. It didn't take long for him to be once again carried away by the feel of her thighs hugging him, the fragrant scent of her perfume, the wet and tight essence of her. He surrendered to all of it, everything that made her Ava.

* * *

"You should get back to the party," she said, curled up against him on the sofa.

"Why?" He asked, moving her hair away from her neck and kissing her shoulder. "Everyone has already congratulated me, and are by now, enjoying the free food and booze." He went silent for a while and then spoke again. "You never cashed the check."

She turned to look up at him with surprise. "How do you know that?"

"My dad told me. He's trying to make amends and told me that even though you took the check, you never cashed it."

She looked away and shrugged. "I never wanted it. I only took it, because I believed the best thing to do was to walk away from you. I never thought we should be together, but I also didn't want to be bought."

He reached his hand under her chin and turned her head back up to look at him. "Why would you let me go on thinking that you were? My father keeping shit from me, I can understand. But you—I always thought I could trust you to tell me everything."

Ava sat up, wrapping his suit jacket around her breasts. "It's not like I wasn't tempted to cash it. The first time I left, I stayed with my parents and when I lost the baby, I didn't care about anything, especially not money. But when I left Gypsy Bay for good and moved to L.A., things were tight money-wise for a while. I made several trips back and forth to the bank to cash it, but I couldn't. Eventually, I just shredded it."

She looked at him just in time to see him chuckle and shake his head in wonder.

"What?"

"We are the most non-communicating people I know," he

said. "Everything you're telling me now, could've been said five years ago."

She scoffed. "When? When I'd left the first time without so much as a goodbye? When I came back and you were married? After your wife was murdered? When was a good time to come back into your life and tell you that I still loved you and that all the bad stuff you thought about me wasn't true?"

He sat up and grasped her shoulders to turn her toward him. "Any time. Any time would've been perfect, because I never stopped loving you or wanting you. I've always wanted you, even throughout high school when you tried to scare me away with that ridiculous tough girl act."

She laughed. "It didn't work. You were never scared of me."

"No, I wasn't." He kissed her softly then pulled back to hold her within his gaze. "But, I was scared of being without you."

She looked away, not knowing what to say to that, but he searched for her eyes again.

"That morning after we made love, you said you would be here," he said.

She nodded. "And you asked me for how long."

"The question still stands."

She stared at him in alarm. "Gabriel—"

"You can't blame me for asking. You left once, came back and left again and each time, it broke me. So, again, for how long?"

"I'm here," she said, speaking and looking at him with all sincerity. "I'm here for as long as we'll have each other. Those years away from you only made me realize how foolish I was. It was hard leaving you. But it was even harder being without you."

When he didn't respond, fear that it may be too late engulfed her. "Do you believe me?"

He still didn't say anything but reached around her to grab something off the end table beside the sofa. When he was once again beside her, she looked down at his hands and saw he was holding a rectangular velvet jewelry case. Ava stared at it like a snake poised to bite her.

"It's obviously not for me, Ava," he said. "Take it."

She swallowed and slowly reached out to take the case from his hands and hesitated a moment longer before finally opening it. When she saw what was inside, she raised her head to look at him with curiosity.

"I noticed you don't wear that gem around your neck anymore."

"The stone cracked when I fell."

He nodded and she saw that he was also, suddenly cautious. "I may be overstepping my bounds here, but I thought that this could replace it."

She looked down again at the thin white gold necklace and lifted it delicately. At the center wasn't a lapis lazuli stone, but what looked very similar to a pearl.

"It's a moonstone," he said.

She shook her head. "I don't understand."

"You said you got pregnant in September and miscarried eight weeks later."

She slowly nodded. "That's right."

"Well, I did the math and figured if everything had worked out and you had a healthy pregnancy, the baby...our baby, would've been born around June."

"That's what the doctor told me."

Gabriel gestured to the necklace awkwardly. "Well, um, that would've been his or her birthstone."

Ava stared, completely speechless and feeling her heart flood with warmth.

"I know it's probably silly," he rushed to say. "I looked it up and at eight weeks, it was no bigger than a kidney bean." He paused. "But it was still something. Something growing inside of you. Something we made together."

She shook her head quickly and the tears that had been building behind her lids spilled over and trailed down her cheeks.

"No, it's not silly at all."

She unclasped it and wrapped it around her neck and tried to fasten it, but the tears were blinding her and the love she felt for him was so overwhelming that she couldn't get her fingers to work. Gabriel moved in, stilled her hands and fastened the necklace for her. When he moved back to look at her, the love she felt for him was overflowing, and she couldn't wait any longer to show him how she genuinely felt. She clasped his face between her hands and placed her lips gently on his. The kiss was tender and spoke of the future she wanted with him. As if in answer, he wrapped his arms around her and returned the kiss, going from tender and sweet to passionate and all-consuming—the way only Gabriel could do.

* * *

Thank you for reading EX APPEAL! If you enjoyed Gabriel and Ava's exciting love story, you'll love the next book in the EX FILES series, EXPOSED.

When married couple Eric and Havilland Sawyer find themselves on opposite sides of a high-profile investigation, what could possibly go wrong?

Everything.

ONE-CLICK EXPOSED NOW >

"A plot twist you do not see coming."

"This book will take you on a ride and just when you think you've figured everything out, she surprises you and takes you in a different direction."

SIGN UP FOR LISA'S NEWSLETTER:

www.lisaryancampbell.com/newsletter

And if you love Christmas with romance and suspense, make sure you check out EX O EX O, my EX FILES Christmas novella.

It's three days until Christmas and Agent Roman Walsh has one assignment: Get Senator McIntyre's ex-wife into protective custody. It's supposed to be a simple job to drive her from California to Washington, and he'll be home in time

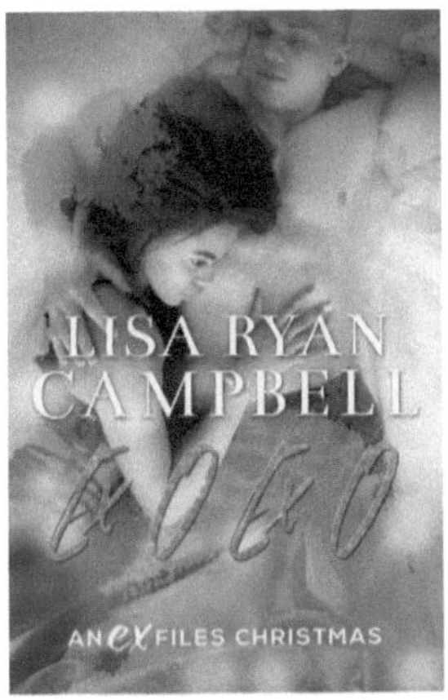

to see his kids on Christmas morning. It's his kids he's thinking about when he secretly accepts money from a mysterious stranger who asks him to take a slight detour in his trip. But what he soon finds out is the money he took comes with strings and will ultimately put his life and the life of the woman he once loved in danger.

Dana McIntyre is in possession of a list that belongs to the Senator, detailing the names of those he accepted bribes from during his term in office. She plans to hand it over to the District Attorney in exchange for protection from some very dangerous people who also want the list and will stop at nothing to get it. When she finds out her escort to Washington is the man who walked away from her years ago, a pain she thought was long gone resurfaces, and she wonders what she has gotten herself into.

With each mile Roman and Dana travel together, they relive memories and buried feelings of a young love that ended too soon. However, they will have to learn to trust each other again if they're going to survive the enemies on their trail and make it to Christmas morning. But that won't be so easy, because one of them has been lying from the very beginning.

. . .

ONE-CLICK EX O EX O and warm up this holiday season with this steamy, suspenseful novella.

The Ex Files

Exiled

Exchange

Explosive

Exposed

Ex Files Box Set

Execution

Extortion

The Ex Files Novellas

Explicit

Ex Factor

Ex O Ex O

Ex Appeal

Historical Romance

Deceit and Seduction

Award-winning Author, Lisa Ryan Campbell began writing as a small child using her mother's pink typewriting paper. Years later, she decided it was important to get a "real job" and attended Arizona State University to major in English with the goal of continuing on for both a Master's and Doctorate degrees in English and teach at the college level.

In 2002, Lisa graduated with a Bachelor's degree in English Literature and an Ancient Egyptian romance novel she wrote in her spare time. She decided then she would not be continuing on to graduate school, but instead joined Romance Writers of America and focused on her true love.

Lisa is an avid traveler and has seen many of the world's treasures in Egypt, Peru, Spain, France, Morocco, England, Mexico and the Caribbean. She spends her time mostly at her home in Colorado writing, reading and watching 1940's noir movies. She also loves to laugh, so you may frequently catch her watching reruns of Archer, Veep and The Office.

Sign up for Lisa's newsletter and find out more about her books at www.Lisaryancampbell.com and connect with her on social media.

www.ingramcontent.com/pod-product-compliance
Lightning Source LLC
Chambersburg PA
CBHW030643190726
48286CB00008B/2635